UNSPOKEN

The Prose Series - Book 1

SOFIA TATE

For A

Always,
S

AUTHOR'S NOTE

Just as parents aren't supposed to admit to having a favorite child, I think the same applies to authors and their novels. But I'm declaring this here and now – UNSPOKEN is my favorite book I've ever written, even though I still have many stories to tell (eight at last count). This book is very different from anything I've written before.

I firmly believe that people enter your life for a reason. For as long as I live, I will always be grateful to the extraordinary person who inspired UNSPOKEN. This person appeared when I least expected it, believes in me when I think I'm a crap writer, and gets excited for me even when I only have "Chapter One" written at the top of the page.

I wrote UNSPOKEN from my heart because of the person who served as its muse. It is the book I was meant to write, and for that and many other reasons, I am thankful for this person's existence and being a part of my life.

AIDEN

I'll never get used to this.

"Yes, Mr. Dwyer, you're expected. Please go right up. Happy holidays!" Isaac, the doorman at 700 Park Avenue, says to me in greeting.

I step into the elevator, then wait as it lifts to the top.

A black-and-white checkered marble floor greets me as I make my way to the sole apartment on this floor.

"Ah, Mr. Aiden, please come in. Let me take your coat," Sinclair, the Parkers' butler, offers when he opens the door of the family's opulent home that takes up an entire floor of the classically designed building, home to many of Manhattan's society families.

After all these years, my heart still races slightly faster and a wave of chills envelops my body, when I step into the apartment of Phillip and Margot Parker, parents of Sebastian Malcolm Parker, my best friend from Princeton.

I am so far out of my comfort zone—the one that will require a ride through the Queens Midtown Tunnel, a zip through the EZ Pass lane, and a couple of exits on the Grand Central to get home tonight.

After handing my coat to Sinclair, I check my jacket and tie in the mirror that hangs in the foyer, even though I already did that in the elevator when I came up; the one with the gold fixtures and Tiffany sconces.

"They're in the living room, sir. Please go right in."

I follow Sinclair's instructions and make my way down the wide hallway, trying not to slip in the new shoes I bought last week for tonight. The maid obviously waxed the floor before I arrived.

I hang a right at the first door, where the sounds of laughter are echoing. Three pairs of eyes turn to me when I step through the doorway.

"Finally!" Sebastian shouts, grabbing me in a tight hug, giving me two hearty slaps on the back, which I return. "What the hell took you so long?"

"It's called traffic, Seb. It happens now and then in Queens. But you wouldn't know since the only time you're in Queens is to catch a flight from JFK or LaGuardia."

"Funny. Let me get you a drink, man."

Seb heads over to the liquor cart to pour me a whiskey when his mother rises from her seat on the sofa.

"Ah, Aiden, so lovely to see you." Sebastian's mother welcomes me in that soft voice of hers, dressed in a red tweed suit and nude stilettos, a glass of pinot grigio in her right hand.

I hand her the box of macaroons I picked up on my way over. "Merry Christmas, Mrs. Parker."

She slaps my arm as if to admonish me. "Aiden, you naughty boy. You know I shouldn't have these."

"It'll be our little secret," I reply with a sly wink.

She laughs at me good-naturedly when Seb's father strides over, his tall frame overtaking his wife's petite form. "Good to see you, Aiden. How's your father?"

I return his handshake. "Thank you, sir. He's well. He gave me this for you, direct from Ireland."

Phillip Parker's eyes glaze over, staring in wonderment at the gift box with *Jameson* emblazoned across the front. "God bless him, son."

I can't help but grin in understanding, knowing well the feeling of the smooth liquor flowing down my throat, giving me a satisfactory burn in return. "I'll tell him."

Seb hands me a crystal tumbler filled with amber liquid. "Here you go, Aid."

"Darling, have you seen the latest issue?" Mrs. Parker asks her son, picking up the most recent issue of *Park* from the coffee table.

"No, Mom," he mutters under his breath with a roll of his eyes.

"You should have a look, dear. It appears several young ladies from your circle are on the committee of that New Year's Eve benefit Bea is working on. So charitable, those girls."

I watch as Seb, with shoulders hunched and emitting a loud sigh, turns toward the Monet hanging over the mantel, as if he's found something fascinating about it that he hasn't before in all the years it's hung in the same place.

During our freshman year at Princeton, Seb filled me in on who his family was—the Parkers of Park Avenue are the family behind *Park* magazine, further going on to explain that it's the magazine for the people in his family's society circle. The only periodical I read on a regular basis is the sports pages in the *Daily News*. The magazine was founded by his grandfather, Hamish Parker, who named it for the street he lived on and where his family still resides, evoking the type of demographic he was aiming for as readers. It also helps that it's a shortened version of the family surname.

Seb's posture echoes the burden he feels carrying on the

family legacy of the magazine. As publisher, Mr. Parker has always hoped that Seb would want to take his rightful place alongside his father at the helm, but his son has zero interest in the magazine. His interests lie more in finding the best places to ski in the off-season, having me play his wingman when he drags me out to some snooty bar on the Upper East Side, and seeing how many phone numbers he can collect on his phone in one night.

Shaking his head in frustration at the sight of his son's disinterest, Mr. Parker leans back in his seat. "So, Aiden, are you working on any exciting sites now?"

I take a swallow of the scotch, turning my attention to Seb's father. "Yes, sir. We've just broken ground on a new apartment building in Long Island City."

"I hear that's a rapidly growing area of Queens."

I nod. "It is. It's our first project that'll be all eco-friendly, collecting rainwater on the roof, solar panels, the whole nine yards. Pop and I are very excited about it."

A low purr fills my ears. "No work boots tonight, Full Ride? Good thing since you could've tracked dirt all over the Aubusson."

Fuck.

I exhale a breath, biting down on the inside of my lower lip. She sounds like honey at first, but then delivers a remark full of tart that causes one to wince in pain.

I stand and turn around, coming face-to-face with the woman who to others may seem like my nemesis by how we address each other, but in reality, she's the object of my lust and affection, and she would say the same if you asked her.

Beatrice Parker, Bea, Seb's little sister, or "The Park Avenue Princess" as local gossip columnists have crowned her. The girl who attended the finest schools, had her debutante coming out ball at the Waldorf, and is now primed to pick a husband only the best money and status can buy. A handful of suitors are already chomping at the bit to be known as Mr. Beatrice Parker.

Good luck, morons. You'll never know how to handle a spitfire like her.

Bea possesses the ability to turn otherwise mature, intelligent men, into babbling masses of drained, brainless flesh.

Except me—Full Ride, the nickname she ungraciously bestowed upon me because I received a full scholarship to Princeton. I never lose IQ points around her. I can give as good as I get, in spite of the heat sparking between us, or maybe because of it.

Here we go. Ready.

"Hello, Buzzy."

I smirk at the frown that takes over her entire face. She loathes it when I call her that. She throws her shoulders back and raises her head.

Aim.

"Aiden. I see you have a beard now. I'm surprised you didn't show up in a flannel shirt. What's next? Moving to a four-story walkup in Williamsburg next to an artisanal cheese shop and an organic free-trade café where you grind your own coffee beans?"

"I trimmed it especially for you, so you wouldn't be repulsed if the sauce from the *duck a l'orange* dribbled into it. And what about you? Will you be terrorizing the other skiers in Aspen for New Year's Eve?"

"Actually, it'll be St. Moritz. After the benefit, of course."

"Good. I'll be sure to warn the Swiss ski patrol to be on the lookout for a five-eight blonde who believes rules don't apply to her."

Fire.

"Don't worry about me, Aiden. I doubt I'll be skiing that much. I'm staying in a chalet that belongs to our close family friends. They want me to meet their nephew. A member of the Lichtenstein royal family. Who knows, I might just come back engaged."

Bullseye.

Her frown is now upturned into a victorious grin.

My hand tightens on my glass. As much as she's won this round, and I'm smarting from her verbal lashing, it doesn't stop me from wanting her. My eyes roam over her lithe body, her jade-green silk dress accentuating her emerald eyes and every luscious curve, the shiny silver heels on her feet highlighting her perfectly formed legs, her blond hair pinned into a bun at the nape of her neck, and finally, the fire engine-red lipstick covering her full mouth.

I press my lips together to keep myself from doing what I want most right now—to drag her into the nearest closet, maid's room, I don't give a fuck as long as it's empty, then keep her there until she admits what I've known for a while now—she wants me too. The Park Avenue Princess and the son of the Irish immigrant construction worker father from Astoria, Queens, who got a full ride to an Ivy League university. If I have to smear her lipstick as I take her tongue into my mouth, or undo that proper bun, letting the pins drop to the floor, cover her neck and chest with soft kisses and long licks, reach under her dress and gently rub her wet pussy with my fingers—I would do it all until she gave in, gave herself to me.

And she knows it, judging by the softened look in her eyes, a look that seems to have cropped up again and again over the past few months as if she's finally noticed me as a man and not just her brother's best friend. If only she weren't my best friend's little sister and so far out of my league that I may as well be the unrequited pool boy at her family's estate in the Hamptons.

"Okay, stand down, you two," Mr. Parker declares, rising

to his feet. "I think dinner should be ready by now. Let's adjourn into the dining room, shall we?"

I don't move, and neither does Bea. Our eyes are locked on each other, our chests rising with each breath, impervious to Seb and his parents grabbing their cocktails and moving toward the door.

A hard slap on my shoulder blade jolts me back. "Come on, Aid. I'm starving. And I'm guessing so are you," Seb surmises.

Too right, man, but not for salad with champagne dressing, roasted goose, or apple pie with vanilla coulis.

Bea gives me one last smirk before turning for the door, her lovely round ass covered in green silk taunting me.

That gorgeous ass. That is why I'm starving.

DINNER GOES AS USUAL IN THE PARKER HOUSEHOLD. FOOD is served to the right of the guest; plates are removed from the left. Various discussion topics are discussed—the stock market, Christmas sales, the family's upcoming winter stay at their home in Lyford Cay.

All polite. All proper.

But the looks that Bea and I exchange when no one is watching are nowhere near close to anything resembling propriety and decorum. She sits across the table from me, the light from the silver candelabra illuminating her creamy skin, highlighting the hints of caramel in her hair. We don't need to verbally spar now. The power of her eyes expresses everything I need to know—she desires me as much as I do her. But I know she will never act on those feelings. I am beneath her in every way that matters to her—financially and socially. Plus, there's Sebastian. Even though it's unspoken between us, we're afraid of what would happen if we acted on our feelings.

She doesn't even have to say it out loud. Goodbye, best friend.

Finally, the meal ends with everyone pushing back from the table, returning to the living room for port or cognac, as is the ritual.

I excuse myself and head for the guest bathroom. Winding my way toward it, I decide to take a detour and explore. I've been here countless times for various occasions, but I'm always blown away by the sheer luxury of my best friend's family home. Nobody would think I was doing something untoward, but if asked, I could always say I was inspecting things from a construction point of view.

I pass by the library, covered in wall-to-wall cherry wood bookshelves, all of them accessorized with sliding ladders to reach the books on the highest level. I step in and admire the quiet solemnity of the space when something catches my eye.

A silver laptop sits alone on a side table near one of the leatherback chairs. I can't help my curiosity. I step over and glance at the screensaver—a picture of Bea with her best friend, Marisol.

It's her laptop.

I really shouldn't.

I glance behind me to make sure I'm alone. I press the screen open.

A page pops up, illustrated in black and gold with the text against a white background. The website's header is in black and written in cursive script: *Prose. For Discreet Singles.*

My eyes pop open in shock. There's no way Seb would need to join a dating site because he can land three girls in one night, which I saw happen more than once when were at school. And neither would Bea because—

Then I see the login box for the user ID and password. The password box is empty, but not the ID. *10280girl.*

Beatrice is the only single girl in the house.

Holy shit. It *is* Bea. On a fucking dating site. What in the hell is she doing on here? The line of her potential suitors could stretch up and down Park Avenue.

I pause when I realize she didn't use her own zip code, 10021.

Where the fuck is 10280? I pull my cell from my back pocket and google it. The result reads Battery Park City, at the southernmost tip of Manhattan.

That makes sense. She finds great pleasure in reminding me that nobody in her social circle ever ventures below 57th Street, except for a Broadway show in Times Square or a trendy restaurant in Soho or Tribeca.

I reach down to click on the other links on her laptop, but before my finger reaches the icon, the sound of high heels walking down the hallway echoes into the room. Thank God for Carrara marble tiles.

I jump back from the laptop and silently beg for the screen to close. I rush over to the display case where the first copy of *Park*, the one that Seb's grandfather produced by hand, sits permanently under glass with an art light over it, illuminating the cover proudly as if it were in a museum. I make it in time to pretend I'm studying the magazine just as Bea enters the room.

"What are you doing in here?" she asks haughtily.

"Why? You miss me?" I counter, still pretending I'm interested in the display.

"Just making sure you weren't casing the place."

I exhale deeply. This woman. I swear...if I could, I'd have her over my knee just like that, and she wouldn't have time to blink before I gave her what we both want so desperately.

I spin around and give her a wicked grin. "If I wanted to rob the place, Buzzy, I would've done it by now. Trust me. I'm smarter than I look."

"You must be if Princeton accepted you."

I turn back to the display case so I don't have to look into the shimmering green pools of her eyes. "Gee, thanks," I throw over my shoulder.

"I mean it."

My brows narrow in confusion at her reply.

I pivot back to her. "Correct me if I'm wrong, but I believe that's the first compliment you've ever given me."

Without warning, her eyes turn soft and warm. "There's a first time for everything," she whispers. The heat in her eyes is unmistakable.

What the fuck? My cock twitches in my pants. I have to leave now before I accept the invitation in her expression, and risk her brother walking in on us.

"See you back in the living room," I reply roughly.

I race for the bathroom, where I splash cold water on my face to cool off. I stare into the mirror, wondering what the hell just happened, and even more than that, why she's a member of an internet dating site.

I throw my shoulders back and adjust my tie.

1028ogirl, brace for impact.

2

BEA

*H*is hands.

God, his beautiful hands.

Those strong, masculine hands running gently over my neck, then slowly unzipping my dress. The silk swooshes quietly to the ground.

Then he unhooks my bra, helping me with the straps, pushing them softly off my shoulders.

And then...the rough, callused tips of his fingers begin to carefully trace the outline of my breasts, discovering their weight, their fullness. His thumbs circle both areolas simultaneously as he licks his lips hungrily, preparing to devour me.

But those fingertips...I don't mind their texture, the rough feel of them. He works with his hands—running a cement mixer, operating a heavy drill, driving a bulldozer.

He is a man in every sense of the word. He doesn't sit behind a desk with a Bluetooth attached to his ear 24/7. His gorgeous physique isn't formed with the help of a personal trainer at the gym, but by hours of hard manual labor that in the end will create a beautiful addition to the New York City skyline.

And then, he leans in closer to me, his mouth open and ready to take me—

"Beatrice!"

I jolt when someone's hand touches my arm.

"Beatrice dear, I believe we lost you there for a moment."

I look over at Mrs. Penelope Covington, the chairwoman of the benefit where I'm serving as head of the planning committee. Dressed impeccably in a dove-gray Chanel suit, the older woman is one of New York City's last society matriarchs. Her white hair is styled in an attractive pixie cut, and her rimless glasses sit on the bridge of her nose.

I clear my throat, turning red at the sea of faces staring back at me, waiting for me to say something. "Forgive me, Mrs. Covington, I was lost in my thoughts."

"Happens to the best of us. Now, how are we coming along with the silent auction items?"

I look over my list. "They're all set. I confirmed with Mom and Dad that I could donate our house in the Bahamas for a seven-day vacation. Seb is giving us a consultation with his Savile Row custom tailor the next time he's over from London."

"Excellent," the older woman remarks.

"I'd love my own personal consultation with Sebastian," Isabella Richmond comments across the table from me.

Do not roll your eyes at her.

I sigh quietly to myself. Isabella lives in my building. Her family can trace their ancestors back to the Mayflower, or so she claims. She's been after Seb practically ever since his voice changed, and he sprouted about three feet. But the truth is that she's not the only one who wants to become Mrs. Sebastian Parker. Any girl between the ages of eighteen and twenty-five from a good society family throws themselves at my brother at every benefit, ball, or dinner party. But my brother will never settle down and have children unless my father gives him his "The Parker name must live on" speech, and to my knowledge, he hasn't yet. But until then, he'll be the number one Manhattan bachelor, perpetually gossiped about on *Page Six*.

I hear a mumbled laugh under someone's breath. I look across to my best friend, Marisol, full name Marisol Evangeline de la Cruz Boudreaux. We met on our first day as high school freshmen at Spence. She laughed out loud when our chemistry teacher shared my response to one of her orientation questions with the class: "When do you perform unauthorized experiments in the classroom?" Using what logic I possessed at the time as a fourteen-year-old girl, I of course replied, "When the teacher is out of the room." The correct answer was "Never." Nobody thought that was funny, except for Marisol, and we've been close ever since.

I look across the table at her. She rolls her eyes at me, indicating that I had indeed done the same subconsciously just a minute earlier, so I need to watch myself around the others, lest I'm caught and my transgression is reported on social media and my reputation as "The Park Avenue Princess" is tarnished. Something I wouldn't mind, if I were to be honest with myself.

"Are we still under budget, Maisey?" Mrs. Covington asks another committee member. "Beatrice, would you kindly double-check the numbers as well?"

"Certainly," I offer, opening my laptop, but I already know that the budget is fine. Instead of pulling up the spreadsheet I made, I open a blank document and begin writing out my next vignette, as I like to call them. I love Prose because there's no expectation of dating or hooking up unless you connect with another person. And my vignettes are all dedicated to one person, the one man who my parents fawn over to his face but would never want for a son-in-law because of his lack of social status. The one who likes to tease me with the moniker he bestowed upon me when I was a snotty eleven-year-old and he was eighteen on his first visit to our family home during Seb's freshman year at Princeton...

I knock once on Seb's door. I can't wait to see my big brother.

I knock again, but louder this time. I open the door, ready to tackle-hug him when I realize there's someone with him. Some tall guy with dark hair and large build. They're playing that stupid Guitar Hero game, acting like total idiots. He's never brought a friend home before. And his friend is taking my brother's attention from me.

"Hey, Seb! You're home!"

"Oh, hey, Bea!" He gestures toward the other guy with his head. "Bea, Aiden. Aiden, my little sister, Bea."

The guy doesn't even have manners to look at me, simply yelling over his shoulder. "Hey."

"Come on, Seb. Take me to Serendipity for frozen hot chocolate."

"Not now, Bea."

"But it's tradition," I counter.

"Kid, don't you have something better to do than hang out with your older brother?" his friend asks rudely.

I instantly hate him.

"Well, he's my brother, and I haven't seen him since Thanksgiving."

"Bea, I'll take you as soon as Aiden leaves, okay? Right now I have to kick his ass."

I look his friend over from the back. He's dressed in jeans and a T-shirt, compared to Seb who's dressed in his usual polo shirt and khakis.

"How did you two meet?" I ask out of curiosity.

"In the laundry room in our dorm," the intruder chimes in. "Your brother Richie Rich here was about to wash his whites with his colors in hot water, so I taught him how to do laundry."

My mouth drops at this revelation. "Seb, that can't be true. You always send your laundry out."

"Times change, sis."

I don't like this one bit.

I stomp to the monitor and stand in front of it. "Serendipity, Seb. Please?"

They both shout at me to move, but I don't care. Noises screech from the speakers. "Ha! Beat you, man!" Seb shouts in victory, raising his guitar high over his head.

"You suck," his friend replies in defeat. But then he turns to me and gives me a once-over. "You know what, kid? I'm calling you 'Buzzy' from now on because you're like an annoying insect that won't go away, no matter how many times you swat at it."

I roll my eyes at him. "Whatever. Seb, let's go."

I walk triumphantly out of the room when I hear Aiden, the intruder, comment to Seb, "Man, she's annoying."

My brother sighs. "You have no idea, dude."

Twelve years later, I still retain the nickname. And as much as I always protest to him that I hate it, I secretly love it because it's something between us, the only term of affection that marks the futility of desiring something more.

And then we had that moment in the library when he took off like a shot after I told him that I already knew he was smarter than he looks. For the first time since I've known him, I was being sincere, and I scared him away.

I've become an expert at pretending when it comes to Aiden, and now, I'm pretending to care about the difference between ivory and alabaster tablecloths as I begin to type away.

Someone ungraciously nudges my chair. "Hey, you."

I look up to see Marisol standing next to me. "Earth to Beatriz. The meeting's been over for five minutes."

I shake my head, smiling at her nickname for me, the Spanish version of "Beatrice." "Sorry," I mumble. "Just finishing up these last notes. What's up?"

Her dark brown eyes study me carefully. "You tell me. My house. *Vamanos!*"

MARISOL CONVENIENTLY LIVES AROUND THE CORNER FROM me on East 69th Street in a gorgeous limestone townhouse. I used to dash over to her place whenever I got into an argument with my parents as a teenager. But they didn't mind so much because it eased their minds knowing where I was and that I was safe.

Once we walk into her house, we stop in the foyer. She calls out, *"Hola! Bonjour!"* echoing two of the three languages she grew up speaking. Before I even take another step, she pulls me back and lifts her nose into the air as if waiting for something to happen...

"As-tu perdu ton esprit? Il n'y a aucun moyen en enfer je voterai pour cela!"

"No soy ese tipo de artista. Mi trabajo es mi pasión. Dile a ese colector idiota si no le gusta, puede devolverlo a mi y lo donaré al MoMa!"

Marisol smiles to herself, shaking her head. We glance at each other, bursting out laughing. With my basic knowledge of French and Spanish, I can tell her father, Etienne Boudreaux, is arguing with one of his brothers and her mother, Paloma de la Cruz Boudreaux, has an issue with her gallery rep.

As a teenager, I always loved coming over to Marisol's house, not just to see her, but also to be around her parents because they are so different from mine. Etienne Boudreaux is the youngest of three brothers whose family owns Boudreaux Oil based in New Orleans. The family legend goes that he met his future wife on a visit to her native Colombia. Etienne's father, Jean-Luc, took his three sons with him for a meeting with Paloma's father, Rafael de la Cruz, a leading Colombian industrialist.

At the meeting in the sumptuous de la Cruz mansion in

Bogotá, Etienne grew bored and decided to explore the house. He heard someone singing behind a closed door, and when he opened it, he found a petite woman wearing a white T-shirt and ripped jeans with silky hair as dark as black ink streaming down her back, sitting at a pottery wheel, simultaneously working and singing something in Spanish.

The floor below him creaked when he took a step toward her. She swung around, fire in her brown eyes at the sight of the stranger, jumped to her feet, and began yelling at him in Spanish.

Etienne didn't understand a word, but it didn't matter. He was in love.

Unbeknownst to her, Paloma, the youngest of Rafael's three daughters, had met her match in Etienne. Both were considered the black sheep of their families because neither were interested in joining their family companies, choosing to follow their own path. Paloma wanted to be an artist, while Etienne's mantra was that of his native New Orleans: *"Laissez les bons temps rouler."*

And they had not just good times, but the best times together. They had two weddings in Colombia and New Orleans, their family companies went into partnership together, Paloma became a famous artist, Etienne joined his family's board of directors, content to live off the dividends from his family's stock options. They settled in New York City so Paloma could be closer to the art world, both of them away from the shadow of their families.

Whereas my parents met at a 4th of July party at the Bathing Corporation in Southampton, which members call "The Beach Club" or how I refer to it: WASP Central.

I wish my eyes lit up or I was inclined to gesture animatedly whenever I talk about my parents the way Marisol does about hers. My childhood was dull and colorless, filled with ballet classes and French tutors, my parents ensuring I would become the perfect society daughter. But then I met Marisol, who made my teenage years bearable.

"Hola, mija," Marisol's mother calls out to Marisol, sweeping into the foyer dressed in a black silk caftan, her dark hair wrapped tightly in a midnight-blue Hermes scarf, feet bare of shoes.

"Hola, Mami," she replies as she envelops her in a tight embrace, kissing both of her cheeks.

Then she turns to me, greeting me the same. "Always so beautiful, Beatriz. *Como estas?"*

"Estoy bien, gracias."

"What happened on the phone?" Marisol asks her mother.

Senora Boudreaux waves her hand in the air. *"Ay, dios mio!"* She then launches into a fiery tirade in Spanish with Marisol nodding her head in comprehension while I can only catch certain words.

"Oh my, what has my beloved in such a tizzy?" a Cajun accent rings out from the top of the staircase.

Tall, blond with hints of salt and pepper at his temples, and dressed in a white button-down shirt and pressed jeans, Marisol's father, Etienne, descends the stairs toward us. He wraps his arm around his wife's shoulders. "I don't like hearing *ma femme* so unsettled. What's happened, *chère?"*

She then turns to her husband, repeating what she just said to Marisol, but not in French or English. Another reason I love Marisol's parents is that they'll speak in their native languages to each other and completely understand what the other one is saying.

He nods his head in understanding, turning to address his daughter and me, giving us each a hug. "Ladies, I think it's time for our siesta."

Reverting his attention back to his wife, he gently takes

her by the shoulders, leading her up the stairs, with her still explaining the situation in Spanish and him nodding away.

I stare after them wistfully. "I want that someday."

"Since when?" Marisol exclaims in my ear.

My mouth drops at her blunt question. "I don't know," I reply truthfully.

She grabs me by the elbow, pushing me to the back of the house. "Right. I'm going to whip up some peach sangria for us, and we're going to talk in the solarium."

"But it's only noon," I counter.

Marisol sighs. "Oh for fuck's sake, Bea. I know they don't teach you this at WASP University, but you're actually allowed to drink at other times during the day besides right before dinner."

I keep silent as Marisol sits me down in one of the bay windows of her family's solarium that opens onto their back garden. I gaze out the window as I hear metal clinking against glass in the kitchen, with my best friend returning soon after, carrying a tray with a tall pitcher of sangria and two empty glasses. I watch as she pours us each a liberal amount of alcohol, settling into the chaise across from me.

"*Salud,*" she toasts us as we clink glasses. I fold my legs under me, leaning my back against the glass window.

"Okay, what's going on?" Marisol begins.

I take a long swallow from my glass. "Have you ever woken up one day and seen things differently, like something that's been in front of your face the whole time and suddenly it all becomes clear to you?"

"Maybe. But I'm not sure where you're going with this."

Neither do I. How do I explain to her that the guy I've loathed for years, the one who I always complain about to her, is now constantly on my mind? I can't even explain it to myself. Is it because he's so different from the men in my circle? That he makes me feel things that no other man I've ever known has brought out in me, and that these feelings both scare me to death and arouse me to the point where I have to remind myself to breathe?

Fuck it. That's another discussion. Save it for later. Try another tack.

"Do you ever feel like you need more?"

"More from what? Life?"

I nod. "Yes."

"Are you kidding? My life is crazy enough as it is. Just look who my parents are. If I ever added something more to my life, I think I'd spontaneously combust. My life is definitely not empty."

"I know, and I'm envious of that. My life is all about benefit committees and making small talk with men who can't discuss something other than their investment portfolio or their annual conundrum if they should summer in Southampton or Martha's Vineyard. Nothing excites me. Nothing inspires me, except..."

I catch myself, worried that Marisol will judge me about Prose.

"Except what?" she squeaks.

I shake my head. "Nothing."

She jumps up from the chaise, rushing over to me. "No, no, no, Beatriz! Spill. I'm your best friend." She takes my hands in hers. "You know you can tell me anything."

I sigh, letting it all out. "All right. I joined an online service for single people. It's called Prose. You don't exchange pictures. You share..."

"What?"

"Sexual fantasies," I whisper under my breath.

Marisol's mouth drops. "You what? Oh my god! The good girl has finally gone bad! I knew you had it in you! How long have you been doing this?"

"About a month."

She slaps my leg. "And you've been keeping this from me all this time? Have you met anyone?"

I smile slightly. "Not yet, but I'm hopeful."

"So that's why you brought all this up with me."

"Yeah. I know it sounds crazy, but I can't be myself with the men my parents steer toward me. And there's something about not being the Park Avenue Princess when I'm on there that's so appealing. On Prose, I'm just a woman with fantasies looking for someone to play them out with me."

"So it's not a dating service?"

"It is, but the site doesn't advertise itself that way. You read other fantasies, and if you connect with someone, then you can become exclusive and your profile becomes private. I don't necessarily want to meet them in person. I just want to have fun. Does that make sense?"

She takes my hands once more. "It totally does. I'm really proud of you, *chica*. You deserve better than some frat boy who's still tied to his family's apron strings. As for the benefit committees, maybe you can volunteer somewhere? You need some excitement in your life."

I nod. "Isn't that the truth?" I take a deep breath. "I'm just glad I finally told you. I needed to talk to someone about this."

"I'm glad too. Who else would you have told except your best friend since high school? And I'm all in."

Marisol's face suddenly changes, her mouth forming a frown.

"What?"

"I am happy for you, don't get me wrong. But I just want you to be careful. This is the internet, after all."

I nod. "I totally understand. Personal pictures aren't allowed on the site. And my user name doesn't give me away."

"What is it?"

"1028ogirl."

Marisol laughs. "Where the hell is 10280?"

"Battery Park City."

"No wonder I didn't know it. It's out of our comfort zone. Good idea." She rises to grab her glass from the side table near the chaise, joining me once more. She raises her glass. "Here's to 10280girl!"

I laugh, toasting with her. "*Salud!*"

❧

When I get home, Sinclair instantly opens the door for me, even though I was halfway through the lock with my key.

"You didn't have to, Sinclair."

"I have the ears of a bat, Miss Beatrice."

"I know, which is how Mom found out about all those nights I snuck home after curfew in high school."

He smiles at me amusedly. "All part of my job, young lady."

I shake my head at him and go to my bedroom. I dump my things on the bed and change into my sweats and slippers, then grab my phone and laptop.

I walk into the dining room where Mom is finishing up her lunch. I lean over and peck her on the cheek. "Hey."

"Hello, sweetheart. You were with Marisol, I'm assuming?"

"You assume correctly."

She takes a sip from her iced tea. "I'm in a rush, dear. Off to my bridge game, and I'm already running late."

"Kick their butts, Mom," I tease her.

She rises from her chair. "Beatrice, it's bad enough you greet me with a 'hey.' Must you also mock the one hobby from which I receive the most pleasure? One does not 'kick butts' in bridge."

I give her a loving smile. "I know. I'm just yanking your chain."

She shivers in fake horror. "I cannot believe you are my offspring. See you for dinner?"

"I'll be here."

She gives me a quick but firm hug and walks out. I head to the kitchen and make myself a cup of Lady Grey tea, carefully carrying the steaming mug with my phone and laptop to the library.

I settle myself into my favorite chair and log into the Prose website. I begin typing where I left off at the meeting

I read it over twice to check for typos and consistency. Then I hit Post, sending it to my profile page.

"Ecstasy" is now live.

I lean back in the leather-worn chair and take a sip of my tea. Putting the cup back on the side table, I close my eyes and drift to sleep, dreaming of Aiden calling me his "good girl."

"ECSTASY"

Wearing nothing but my Agent Provocateur silk stockings and Christian Louboutin "Pigalles," I present myself to you, reveling in your reaction, feeling the sexiest I ever have in my life.

Kissing you with our tongues tangling as you have taught me, following your direction because I'm always a good girl. Licking your sculptured abs, nuzzling my nose against them. Taking your cock in my mouth, moaning from the pleasure of doing this for you. Being bound at the wrists, with my eyes covered, turning wet at the anticipation of what you will do to me, my heart pounding inside my chest from the unknown. Your mouth feasting on my breasts as you mark me with your teeth.

Your warm breath trails over my body as you finally reach my bare pussy. You alternate between finger-fucking me and sucking on my clit as I writhe and clench the sheets with my fists, begging for you to let me come.

Your glorious cock inside me, pounding me, pummeling so hard and so deep, my entire body bucking, my muscles gripping your shaft so tightly, and then...fuck...I scream your name as I come so damn hard and you fill me with your cum.

The rasp of your voice in my ear calling me your good girl, your warm breath sending shivers up and down my body as I smile in return, knowing I have pleased you, Sir.

3

AIDEN

Taking a long sip from the fourth cup of coffee I've had since this morning, I carefully study the blueprints again. Sitting in the construction trailer in Long Island City where my dad and I are working on our latest building, I make it a point to know every single inch of it to ensure everything is up to spec and there are no screw-ups.

The door opens letting in a whoosh of cold air. Joe, our foreman who's worked for Dwyer Construction for twenty years, stomps his work boots on the floor and heads straight for the Mr. Coffee machine. He pulls off his heavy gloves, grabbing a mug and pouring himself a cup, instantly wrapping his hands around it.

"Fuck, it's freezing out there! Look at you, all cushy in here."

Everyone gives me shit for being the boss's son, but I know it's all good-natured ribbing.

"Don't you think someone should know how to put Nail A into Divot B?"

"Wiseass."

"How's Tommy working out?"

"Not bad, I guess." Joe shrugs.

The second those words come out of his mouth, the growling sound of a bulldozer suddenly cuts out.

"Ah, hell," Joe murmurs. "That's number three."

He puts down his coffee and rushes outside, with me right behind him, pulling on my Carhartt jacket, hardhat, and gloves, grabbing a megaphone.

My father insisted on giving his nephew, Tommy, my uncle Danny's kid, a chance. He was the perfect choice, seeing as he has absolutely zero experience in construction. But he was being way too gentle with the bulldozer, and for us, time is money.

Joe starts to wave his arms to Tommy to get down, but he can't hear a damn thing over the drills and cement mixers. I turn on the megaphone. "Tommy, get down here. Now."

The kid looks like someone just told him Santa Claus doesn't fucking exist. I don't have time for this. "Joe, take over, yeah?"

"No prob. You need to find another job for him."

"Yeah, no shit. Mixing cement shouldn't be too hard, right?"

He gives me a look before heading up to the cab of the dozer. Tommy jumps down, completely dejected.

I pat him on the shoulder. "It's okay, man. You gave it a shot. Want to give the cement guys a hand?" I ask, pointing to our crew next to the mixers.

He nods his head slowly. "Sure."

I walk him over and introduce him to the crew. They look at him suspiciously, but since I'm the boss's son, they welcome Tommy, albeit reluctantly, and begin to point out how the mixture is made.

I sigh to myself and head back to the trailer. I check my watch. Almost time to go home, and I smile to myself because as much as I love my job that's kept me insanely busy since dinner with the Parkers yesterday, I'm aching to get home for one reason—to finally meet 10280girl.

◈

Two hours later, I pull into my driveway in Astoria. I grab my phone and slam the door of my truck shut, beeping the locks.

My dad and I share a two-family house with my uncle Danny, Aunt Rose, and their four kids—Tommy, Patrick, Siobhan, and Danny Jr. I'm an only child, but it never bothered me since I always had my cousins next door to hang out with if I was bored.

I slam my boots against the mat to knock off the dirt and snow before I walk into the house. "Pop?"

"Kitchen, son."

I leave my boots inside next to the door, hanging my jacket on the coat rack. I trudge to the back of the house, finding my dad sitting at the table, eating some kind of meat and potatoes. "Damn, that looks good."

"Aunt Rose brought it over. Leftovers."

"Bless her."

"How was the site?"

I sigh in exasperation. "I still can't believe you gave Tommy a job. Construction is definitely not in his future."

"He's family, Aiden. That's good enough for me."

I shake my head, grabbing a plate from the cabinet, when I spot a paper bag from the pharmacy on the counter. "How was your appointment with the doctor?"

"Eh, same old shite. 'You work too much; you drink too much.' What does that quack expect? I run a construction company and I'm Irish. Comes with the territory."

"Don't you want to live long enough to meet your grandkids?"

He looks over his shoulders in both directions as if he were searching for someone. "You'd better get on that, since I don't see any running around here now."

"Funny, Pop." I sit down and heap a huge portion of roast beef and potatoes onto my plate, shoveling a forkful into my mouth.

"Speaking of, how's Beatrice?"

My mouth instantly stops chewing at the sound of her name. "Why?"

"You never told me how dinner went with her and her family."

I start chewing again. "Fine," I mumble with a mouth full of food.

The room turns silent, unnerving me. When I look up from my plate, my father is staring right at me. "What?"

"First, don't talk with your mouth full. I raised you better than that. Second, I asked because usually you come home ranting about the latest jibe she took at you, but this time, not a damn peep. What happened?"

"Nothing happened."

"Don't bullshit me, Aiden."

I put down my fork. "Fine, since you asked." I pause. "She was nice to me."

His eyebrows lift in surprise. "She was *nice* to you?"

"Yeah, and it fucking threw me off. Scared the shit out of me, to be perfectly honest."

A huge smile takes over my father's face. "I see."

Now my curiosity is piqued. "What does that mean?"

"Your ma, God rest her soul, hated my guts at first too. But then, well, you know..." His eyes light up at the memory.

My heart stops when I see his eyes glaze over. "It's okay, Pop. Go on."

"When she came to see me in the hospital after I had that emergency appendectomy back in my twenties, I asked her why she was here and she said, 'To make sure you're still alive. You scared the crap out of me.' Even though she said it like it was no big deal, I could tell she was afraid she was going to lose me. And that's how I knew."

We simultaneously look at the refrigerator door where three pictures hold a permanent place—me with Pop and Ma when I was born, one from their wedding day, and her graduation picture from Hunter College where she studied to be a kindergarten teacher. And above them, her prayer card from her funeral with her name across the top, Maeve McLoughlin Dwyer.

Pop takes a long swig from his beer. He puts down his glass and looks me straight in the eye. "Son, if you care for that girl even one ounce of what I felt for your ma, do something about it because life is just too fucking short."

I stare back at him just as determinedly. "Already on it, Pop."

He pats my hand. "Good boy."

Pop pushes back from the table, carrying his plate to the sink. I watch him leave, then quickly finish my dinner because, like he said, life is just too fucking short.

AFTER WASHING OUR DINNER DISHES, I TAKE A QUICK shower to get the dirt and sweat off me. Wrapping myself in a towel, I pour myself a whiskey, carrying the tumbler into my room. I shut the door, then sit down at my desk and turn on my desktop.

Hurry the fuck up.

Finally, I'm online. I click onto the Prose website and sign up for the free membership, giving myself a second to think of a user ID that won't give away my identity. I fill out the usual profile questions about age, height, eye and hair color, again using the opposite of what each one really is, except for gender.

I click on the "About" page. What the...

"Prose is an online site like no other. We are dedicated to serving the needs of singles who have no interest in sharing their pictures or biographies. Instead, our members share their ultimate sexual desires and fantasies with one another. Prose caters to all sexual orientations – in our opinion, love is love.

NOTE: Before you join, you must agree to adhere to our zero tolerance policy on abuse, harassment, and non-consent, which can be found on the 'Become a Member' page."

Holy shit.

Buzzy, how in the fuck did you find this place? And why the fuck are you on it?

I continue reading over the website's features— only written prose is allowed, but you can IM with other members if they're online.

I search the membership rolls for her. Finally, I spot her ID.

I grin to myself.

Found you, baby. Now let's see what you don't want anyone to know. Let me meet the real you.

According to her profile, she's only written two pieces. I click on her latest one that she titled "Ecstasy."

I start to read her words. What the...my eyes widen.

I can't believe...my cock grows harder with each line I read.

Oh, baby...

My Bea, my Buzzy...

So much I didn't know about you.

Untying the towel from my waist, I start to reread it. I reach for my dick, slowly stroking it.

I want to see you in those stockings and stilettos, baby. Just for me. While I'm sitting in my desk chair, wearing nothing but my worn jeans.

I won't tie you up at first because I want to feel your nails scoring the flesh on my back.

I hold my cock tighter as it grows swollen to the point of pain.

I will devour your tits, Beatrice. Suck on them so hard that I'll make you come from that alone. Stretch out your nipples with my teeth, mark you as I bite them because you are mine. You will carry my mark with you.

I pump my shaft faster and faster...

I'm fucking you, baby. Fucking you so hard and rough. You're screaming "Yes!" and then I command you to say my name, and you do so obediently because you are my good girl.

I explode all over my torso, coating my abdomen with my cum. I fall back into my chair, panting hard. I use the damp towel to wipe myself off. I rise on shaky legs to my feet, putting on a fresh T-shirt and pair of boxers.

Still standing, I stare back at the screen, my chest still rising and falling rapidly.

I sit back down and begin to write.

You don't know it yet, but you will be mine very soon, baby. All mine.

❦ 4 ❦

BEA

*Y**ou have a message from GalwayPlayer,* the email message from Prose reads when I open the Mail app on my phone.

My heart starts to beat faster from the first reply I've received since joining the site.

I begin to read his profile.

Galway...Irish. Nice.

Player. Either he's a manwhore or he's into sports. I hope it's the latter.

Heading down the hallway to the foyer, I smile widely to myself, about to open the message when my father's voice jolts me, forcing me to look up.

"Sweetheart, what has got you beaming so much that you're practically glowing?"

I shake my head dismissively. "Oh, it's nothing. Just some good news about the benefit. The florist we wanted gave us a reasonable quote."

I look behind my father to see my mother giving instructions to our maid in the living room. I notice the coffee table is covered in crystal vases of fresh flowers, as are the mantel and side tables.

"Dad, what's going on?"

He looks at my outfit before replying. "Are you going somewhere?"

I pull tighter on my coat and scarf, suddenly hesitant to answer. "I wanted to see the Canaletto exhibit at the Met before it closes on Sunday. Is there a problem?"

He purses his lips. "I need you to stay home this morning. The Thornes are coming over."

I sigh in disappointment. "Porter Thorne's parents?"

"And Porter, which is why I'd like you here."

Porter Thorne. God give me strength. The kid who always stepped on my toes when we were thrown together at the Knickerbocker Cotillion dancing lessons that my parents forced me to attend when I was a kid. The pimple-faced geek whose hair was always falling in his face and nose was always running. I heard he ended up at MIT, but beyond that, I don't know what he's up to now.

The sound of the doorbell breaks the silence between my father and me.

I guess I'm about to find out.

Sinclair opens the door to reveal the Thorne family—Gregory Thorne, one of the hedge fund kings of Manhattan, Meredith Thorne, one of the society queens of the Upper East Side, and following close behind, their only child, Porter.

I'm stunned by what I see. Though his hair is still floppy, I see no evidence of any pimples. He's actually...okay looking. Not my type at all, though. He could pass for Chris O'Donnell's younger brother. But he's too clean-cut for me. I doubt he could keep up with me. Not like Aiden...

Do not think about him.

"Hi, Beatrice."

Porter's voice snaps me back to attention. "Hi, Porter. It's been a long time."

He smiles at me. "I know." He takes note of my coat and gloves. "Were you on your way out?"

I nod. "Yeah, but my dad asked me to stay. I have no idea why."

"Same here. My parents asked me to come down from Boston for this."

We stare at each other, not in an aroused manner, but more as if we've just realized something is about to happen unbeknownst to us and we're both scared to death.

My mother's cheery voice wafts over us. "Come, everyone. Let's go inside, shall we?"

A wave of chills comes over my entire body.

A lamb to the slaughter.

Once inside, Porter and I greet each other's parents as Sinclair takes my coat and scarf. Drinks are served.

"Sweetheart, take the loveseat with Porter," my father insists.

I exchange confused looks with my former dance partner. Once I sit down, I have to place my hands on my knees to keep them from shaking.

My father clears his throat. "Beatrice, you are aware that *Park* isn't doing well financially with the advent of digital. Our print sales are down dramatically."

I tilt my head at him. "I know that, Daddy. I read our financials every quarter. It's worrying to be sure."

"Unfortunately, the old guard is getting too old," my father continues. "The younger generation just isn't interested in reading print anymore. We will need to deeply invest in transitioning to a digital platform."

I nod. "That makes sense. And I know that it's my family legacy, but I'm not quite sure what this has to do with me.

You said you always wanted Sebastian to join you at the magazine."

My father clasps his hands together. "This is true, and at some point, once he gets over his playboy antics, I'm sure he will. But I don't know when that will happen, and we need the cash now to go digital."

"Which is where I come in," Gregory Thorne chimes in without warning.

"Well, I'm certainly grateful to you for that, Mr. Thorne. But I'm still confused about why we're here," I reply, gesturing to Porter and myself.

"Beatrice, dear..." my mother starts, then shifts her eyes between Porter and me. "We had an idea that perhaps the two of you could get to know each other better."

My mouth drops. She's kidding, right? This cannot be happening. Porter and I turn our heads toward each other, the shocked look on his face mirroring my own.

"Dad?" he asks his father for confirmation of his fears.

Mr. Thorne clears his throat. "Look, son, you're not getting any younger. And investing in a magazine is a high-risk venture. I have a board of directors to answer to. If the two of you were married, there's less of a chance that the board will balk at the idea of this partnership."

My head begins to spin from the sound of the words...*partnership, married.*

I jump to my feet, my legs shaking from the shock. "Are you kidding me? For crying out loud, this is not the nineteenth century! I have my own life. In this century. I'm not going to marry someone for the sake of a fucking business deal!"

"Beatrice, language!" my mother admonishes me.

"Mom, Dad, I'm sorry. But there's no way in hell I'm going through with this." I turn to Porter. "I'm so sorry you were dragged into this. I meant no offense."

He shakes his head at me. "Don't worry. None taken."

I yank my purse from the floor and storm back to my room. I slam the door behind me, collapsing onto my bed. I clench my hands, trying to get a grip on myself. My breathing comes so fast that I think I'm going to hyperventilate. I stare across at my bookshelf filled with my Austen and Brontë favorites when it hits me...

Prose.

I haven't read the message yet.

I quickly grab my bag and rummage through it for my phone. I swipe until I get to the Prose app, opening it as fast as I can. I click on the Message icon, revealing the message from GalwayPlayer.

Hello, beautiful.

I'm new here. I was greatly attracted to your prose.

I would love to be your guide as you explore your desires with me. I will please you until you come so hard that you see stars behind your eyes and beg for mercy. I will worship your soft flesh, making you feel like the most desired woman on the planet. But I will also insist that you submit to me so my own desires are fulfilled. To hear you call me "Sir" and to be able to call you my "good girl"—that is what I want from you, until we are both spent and sated.

I will start by asking for two things, my good girl. The first - tell me something about yourself that no one knows. The second - tell me something you want that you're too afraid to ask for.

Yours,

GalwayPlayer

My hands shake as my mouth forms a wide smile. A guide? Someone who could help me figure out what I truly want without revealing my true identity? Yes. This is what I want. What I need.

But now…how do I put off my family?

A gentle knock on the door snaps me back. I drop the phone onto my bed, rubbing my eyes with the backs of my hands. "Come in."

My father's face appears in the doorway, stern and determined. "Beatrice, I understand that you're a bit blindsided by this."

I laugh to myself. "'A bit?'"

"We're not mandating that you marry anyone, but do you think you could just give Porter a chance?"

Do I have a fucking choice?

He continues in the face of my silence. "Losing the magazine would be an enormous blow to all of us. I would be fine, but your mother and Sebastian…They don't know anything else but this life."

The guilt card. *Well played, Daddy.* "Of course. Give me a moment."

"Thank you. I'll see you shortly."

He gently shuts the door behind him. I step into my en suite bathroom to check my face. I pour myself a glass of water from the tap, letting the cool liquid soothe my throat. I check my face, reapplying my lip gloss. I look myself over once more and grab my purse, heading for the living room. GalwayPlayer is going to have to wait until after lunch.

As I join my parents and the Thornes, I stop suddenly when I see Porter dressed once again in his coat, pulling on a pair of brown leather gloves.

"What's going on?" I ask.

My mother rises to her feet from her place on the sofa. "Dear, we thought perhaps you and Porter should have some time to yourselves. We know this proposition may have come as a bit of a shock to you."

May have?

I exhale a deep breath. Porter steps toward me. "We could

get some coffee. You probably know where to go around here."

I tilt my head at his warm tone and nod. "I do."

I turn around to see Sinclair already standing in the hallway, holding my coat, scarf, and gloves. I quietly thank him.

"I'm ready," I announce to the group.

Porter joins me at my side, turning back to address our parents. "We'll be back soon."

"Take your time," Mrs. Thorne shouts out to us.

"We'll see you soon," Mom adds.

Porter sighs audibly, while my own teeth clench at the happy tone in their voices.

Sinclair holds the door open for us. Waiting for the elevator, neither Porter nor I exchange a word. The silence is stifling.

"Let's go to Nespresso," I suggest, desperate to make some kind of noise to break up the bundles of nerves in my stomach.

"That's fine," he replies with no hint of emotion.

Outside my building, I lead us south down Park, then west to Madison and 65th. We enter the café, where the space buzzes with a cacophony of voices, holiday shoppers, and tourists speaking in various accents.

Once seated, I order a vanilla latte, while Porter orders an espresso. The waitress walks away, and we finally look straight at each other

"So..."

"So..."

"This isn't awkward," I observe.

"Not in the slightest," he jokes. "What were they thinking? I have my own life that doesn't revolve around charity balls and cocktail parties." He stops for a second, realizing what he said. "Sorry. I didn't mean—"

I shake my head. "I wasn't insulted. That's what my life

revolves around, and sometimes it feels incredibly claustrophobic."

He nods in acknowledgment as our drinks are set down in front of us. "That's how I felt growing up in that environment. The only good thing about it was you."

I stop in mid-sip at his words. "It was? Me?"

"The last time I saw you was at your debutante ball at the Waldorf. And I asked you to dance."

"And you stepped on my feet again. Just like you did when we took those dancing lessons."

"I wanted to get your attention."

"Why on earth would you do that?"

"Because I liked you."

My eyes widen in shock. "You did?"

He looks down at his coffee. "Yeah, but you were so popular, and I was too shy to make a move."

I swallow. "Porter, you're very sweet, but we can't be together because of a childhood crush. We don't know anything about each other. Are you even attracted to me?"

His face goes downcast, eyes on the table. "Yeah," he mutters under his breath. "I had no idea my parents were going to pull this on me. I didn't know anything about the partnership. But I've always had a crush on you. If I were married to you, I could put up with the balls and parties. It wouldn't be the worst thing in the world."

Oh, hell. Go gently.

I reach for his hand. "Porter, look at me."

He finally looks up from the table.

"Thank you. I appreciate that. I truly do. I wish I could say the feeling was mutual. You deserve to be with someone who loves you unconditionally and makes you happy."

"I agree, but what do we do about our parents?"

I sigh in desperation. "I have no clue. If we tell them outright we won't do it, then they'll just keep nagging us.

Maybe we should just play along until they get over this ridiculous idea. Pretend we like each other."

His mouth quirks in contemplation. "That could work, I suppose. It's not like we would encroach on each other's lives since we live in different cities. We'll just see each other when it's necessary."

"Exactly. We'll have to work together on this so our parents buy that we're into each other."

He nods. "I hope we can pull it off."

"Me too."

Suddenly, the wheels start turning in my head. Who do I know in my circle that would be interested in *Park*, investing in it, writing for it, editing it, bringing it into this century? I'll have to ask Marisol what she thinks.

My other goal is to get to know a man named Galway-Player and figure out exactly what I have to do for him to call me his "good girl."

❦ *5* ❦

AIDEN

"**C**ome on, Mikey, get your ass in the game!"

From my position as goalie, I watch as the star forward on Dwyer Construction's amateur soccer team completely misses the opposing goalpost by a yard. He barely managed to get his foot on the ball, falling over himself like a klutz.

I shake my head and sigh in frustration. I usually look forward to these games, but this is the second time we're playing Matteo Brothers, and I'm determined to beat their asses. It would diminish the sting of losing to them last time in a 3-0 shutout, most of it being my fault, seeing as I'm the team goalie.

I give the clock a quick glance, exhaling in relief that it's almost two minutes until halftime.

Out of the corner of my eye, I spot a flash of red. Sebastian greets my dad in the bleachers, then sits down in the first row next to him, but what I don't expect to see is Bea greeting Pop with a hug and a peck on the cheek, then taking a seat between him and Seb. I'd invited Seb to the game, but seeing Buzzy here in a long red wool coat, her long, swanlike neck wrapped in a black-and-white checked scarf...

A whizzing sound suddenly flies right past my head, the sound of the ropes in the goalpost cradling the ball.

Cheers erupt from the stands where the Matteo fans sit, as the players begin to whoop and holler for their goal.

"Looks like I'm not the only one who needs to get his ass in the game," Mikey mutters under his breath as he brushes past me.

The whistle sounds, marking the end of the first half. Thank fucking God.

I hustle over to the team bench, grabbing a water bottle and a clean towel, avoiding the angry stares of my teammates. I chug the water, wrapping the towel around my neck as I head over to the stands.

"You asleep there, son?" Pop teases me.

"Something like that," I murmur under my breath, my eyes not leaving Bea because of her demeanor, which has totally thrown me.

She isn't holding her head high, no smirk of any kind across her lips; in fact, she is not giving off her usual haughty manner at all. Instead, she looks almost shy, with her shoulders hunched, looking at anyone and anything but me.

"What's wrong, Buzzy? Looking for your Uber driver to get you back to civilization?" I prod her to get some iota of recognition from her.

"No. I'm sorry you missed that kick," she replies timidly with the shortest of glances in my direction.

What in the hell?

I manage to keep my mouth shut and not let it drop open from the shock of her words.

No snide remarks. No insults. Something is going on.

"Come on, love. I'll get you some hot chocolate," my

father offers, stepping closer to Bea and wrapping his arm around her shoulders as he leads her toward the team bench.

Seb nudges me, joining me to watch them walk away. "Your guess is as good as mine, man."

"What the hell is up with her? I gave her an opening and she just ignored it."

Seb shrugs his shoulders. "No fucking clue. Dinner last night was subdued, to say the least. Nobody was talking. I almost joked about getting someone pregnant just to get a rise out of my parents, but I kept my mouth shut. And when I asked Mom later, she totally brushed me off and said 'Ask your father.' So I did, but he shot me down too. Bea didn't say a word during the ride over either."

My brows narrow in confusion and concern. "Huh. She didn't even complain about being forced to go all the way out to Queens to see me play in some stupid soccer game?"

Seb shakes his head silently.

This isn't my Buzzy.

I thought she'd at least have a certain look in her eyes after the message I sent her, as if she were floating on air or even a hint of lust, some crap like that. But it's as if she's dead behind those beautiful emerald eyes of hers.

I catch my dad and Bea heading back over when an idea pops into my head.

Don't worry, baby. I'm here for you.

Holding onto a steaming Styrofoam cup as if her life depended on it, Bea positions herself next to her brother, taking a short sip of liquid.

"Hey, Buzzy, I was just talking to Seb about him coming out to the worksite to see how the building is coming along, but he can't make it on Monday. Maybe you'd be interested? You have a great eye for style and design. I'd love to hear your thoughts on the project."

I give Seb a just-play-along-and-don't-fuck-this-up glare, with Seb nodding in understanding.

"Yeah, I've got a squash game at the club that I can't get out of," Seb adds. "Why don't you go?"

My heart stops as I wait for her answer.

Bea gives a quick nod. "Sure. I would enjoy that," she accepts with a genuine smile.

She turns back to my father to say something as Seb's eyes widen in surprise and mouths "thank you" at me.

"Anytime," I answer.

If he only knew the lengths I would go to for his sister to see her smile...

6

BEA

I can't help but laugh and roll my eyes at the sight of Aiden standing at the entrance of the building site on Monday afternoon, a pink hardhat dangling from his fingers and a knowing smirk plastered across his lips.

I love how he loves to tease me.

I shoo away the butterflies in my stomach, wishing he didn't make me smile so easily. It would make my life much less complicated.

Shake it off, Bea. Put your game face on.

"Pink? Really? Isn't that a bit sexist?"

"Buzzy, who do you think works here? Members of the *Social Register*? These are construction guys. Union guys. Teamsters. The term 'politically correct' isn't exactly a part of their daily vernacular."

I grin at this realization, something that never would've crossed my mind because I wouldn't have known this on my own. Aiden keeps it real for me, and it doesn't seem to bother him. It's almost as if he enjoys spending time with me, teaching me about his world.

After all these years, after all the insults and barbs, could he really want me? The real me? Well, it's too late now since it looks like my family has no qualms telling me how I'm going live my life as Mrs. Porter Thorne.

"Bea?"

The concern in his voice makes me shiver when I look back at him. His head tilts at me in curiosity. "What's wrong?"

I shake my head, plastering a fake smile on my face. "Nothing. Come on. Show this Park Avenue Princess what it's like to have a real job."

He laughs. "Okay. Let's do it."

I watch as Aiden plants the hardhat on my head with a huge smile on his face. He pulls out his phone to snap a quick picture. "I promise I won't send this to *Page Six*."

"I'll allow it only because I'd sue your Irish ass if you did."

"Duly noted."

He clicks once, runs his fingers over the screen a few times, then I hear a beep on my own phone. I pull it out, seeing the picture appear. "Not bad. Wait...How did you get my number?"

"One, thank you. Two, Seb, who else?"

Of course.

"Come on. I can't wait for the crew to meet you."

He shoves his phone in his back pocket. Guiding me with his hand on my lower back, he steers me inside.

The whoops and catcalls from men standing on the beams startle me, but Aiden rubs my back reassuringly. "Don't worry, they're all good guys. I've got your back, Buzzy."

My face turns warm at his comfort, and I give the workers a quick wave. They promptly return the gesture.

A tall man with a weathered face wearing a hardhat plastered with *Union Now. Union Forever* stickers lumbers over to us. "Hey there. I'm Joe, the foreman. The kid mentioned you'd be visiting."

I'm suddenly touched by this knowledge. I put out my hand in greeting. "Hello. I'm Beatrice Parker. So, you call Aiden 'the kid,' then?"

"Among other things I'd rather not mention in front of a lady."

I blush at his comment.

Aiden grabs my hand, steering me away from the older man. "So let's not tempt him, shall we? Come on, let's get you some tea."

"Lovely to meet you, Joe," I yell over my shoulder.

"Likewise, my lady," he shouts back in reply, then I hear, "Tommy, what the fuck are you doing?"

I laugh under my breath as Aiden simply shakes his head. "Welcome to my world."

He opens the door to the trailer for me as I step in. Various permits are taped to the wall. Filing cabinets, a desk, and a table where blueprints are laid out occupy the rest of the space.

"Have a seat," he offers, gesturing to the high stool next to the table. "Coffee? Tea?"

"I'd love some tea, please."

"With two sugars."

"Yes, please."

My hands freeze on the table. How did he know that?

I dismiss the question from my head, gently fingering the drawings in front of me, taking in the measurements, the terms, the clean lines, the Dwyer Construction logo stamped at the bottom along with the name of the architectural firm.

Aiden appears next to me with a steaming mug. "Here you go."

I gently take it from him. "Do you know what all this means?"

"Yeah, of course," he replies, almost in surprise.

"I'm sorry. I didn't mean to imply—"

"No worries, Buzzy. Would you like me to explain what you're looking at?"

I smile at his easy manner. "Please."

As I take a sip of the tea, Aiden steps closer to me and begins to go over everything, from what certain terms mean to what the end result will look like.

I can't help but lean more into him, eager to make sure I don't miss anything he's saying because I'm genuinely interested. Granted, I was taken aback at first by the size of the site, the noise, the mud, all of the equipment, but when I glance over at Aiden, I glean a sense of pride from how he talks about the building, and before, how he referred to the men on his crew, men that he's probably known since he was a boy. And suddenly, I'm envious of him, because I don't think I've ever experienced that feeling before, that sense of loyalty and family created by a group of men who aren't related by blood.

"So, hopefully, nothing will go wrong, and in the end, we'll have something new and beautiful to contribute to New York City."

"It'll be gorgeous, I'm sure."

"Would you like to have dinner with me?"

I do a double-take, my head pivoting to him.

You're getting too comfortable. Say no, say no.

"Where do you suggest? Balthazar or Le Bernardin?"

He smirks at me. "Well, Buzzy, seeing as I left my dinner jacket at home, I thought I'd take you to Flanagan's, the best Irish pub in Astoria."

"Well, if that's my only option, I suppose I have no choice. Flanagan's, it is then. Do we need to call ahead?" I tease him.

He shakes his head at me. "Buzzy, Buzzy, Buzzy. Why don't you do me a favor and finish your tea while I go out to check on the men and then make sure the passenger seat in my truck is clean enough for your hoity-toity ass?"

"That sounds like a fine idea. Please see to that, will you?"

As I take another sip of my tea, I notice a sudden silence in the room. When I look over at Aiden, his blue eyes are illuminated like an indigo sky, searing into mine. A chill envelops my entire body.

"Be right back," he whispers, a husky tone to his voice.

I watch as he walks out the door. I hold tighter onto the warm mug, desperate to be rid the shivers that have overtaken me.

What the hell am I doing?

AIDEN GRABS MY HAND AS HE LEADS ME INTO FLANAGAN'S. It's what I would expect—a huge crowd, lots of noise and dark wood, and Irish flags hanging everywhere.

"Don't worry, Buzzy. I've got you," he rasps into my ear.

Don't ever let me go.

I give my head a quick shake to rid that thought from my head, afraid of where such a thought would come from and what it means.

He elbows his way toward the back of the pub, finally finding a table for two in the corner.

Aiden pulls back a chair for me. "Thank you," I whisper, not even sure he can hear me over the cacophony.

A petite brunette appears at our table, pad in hand. "Hey, Aiden. What can I get you?"

"Hi, Fiona. Guinness for me. Tanqueray and tonic for the lady, and we'll have two orders of fish and chips."

The woman jots down our order on her pad. "You got it."

He knows the gin I prefer, just like he knew how I take my tea.

The butterflies reappear. I'd give anything for a huge net at this point for my damn stomach.

"Something interesting there?"

I glance up from my clasped hands on the table to a quizzical look on Aiden's face as he gestures to them. "You worried you broke a nail at the site?"

I smile back. "No. I'm just surprised you knew which gin to ask for."

He leans into me, almost too close for my liking. "Buzzy, how long have I known you?"

"Twelve years."

"Exactly. Let's just say I've learned a thing or two about you in that time period."

"What else do you know about me?"

A knowing grin crosses his face. "I'm not telling."

With our elbows touching and his breath wafting over my face, Aiden's blue eyes start doing that thing again—staring into mine so hard that I can sense myself turning wet.

Without warning, GalwayPlayer's message pops into my head, how aroused I was by his words, his promises.

How can two different men have the same effect on me?

We both jolt in our chairs when Fiona reappears with our food and drinks. "Here you go."

I don't even realize how hungry I am until the smell of the battered fish and crispy chips fills my nose.

I reach for the bottle of malt vinegar from the condiments sitting on the table and begin to pour it generously over the fish.

I catch a glimpse of Aiden staring at me again confusedly. "What?"

"Nothing. I thought you'd reach for the tartar sauce instead of the vinegar."

"So I guess you don't know everything about me, do you, Aiden Dwyer?"

"I guess not, Beatrice Parker." He lifts his beer. *"Sláinte."*

Smiling, I clink my gin and tonic with his glass.

We dig into our food, Aiden finishing his much faster than me. Once our plates are taken away, I lean back from the table, taking another sip of my drink.

"Full?" Aiden asks.

"Yes, actually. I can't remember the last time I ate that much."

"More of a salad woman, right?"

I shake my head at him in disappointment. "I must be one big stereotype to you if that's what you really think."

Without warning, his large hand clasps my wrist. "Bea, I was only teasing. Come on. You'd usually give it right back to me. What's going on with you?"

I swallow. "Have you ever felt trapped?"

His eyes bore into me worriedly. "What do you mean by 'trapped'?"

Don't tell him. He'll never understand. He'll just take pity on me. I don't need that. And he's Seb's best friend.

I look away from him. "Nothing. It doesn't matter."

Suddenly, his warm left hand envelops my right. "Hey. You know you can tell me anything," he insists.

Shit. Why did I say anything at all?

The feedback of a microphone jolts us both. "Good evening, everyone. We're 'A Family of Finians.' Let's see how much we can fill up the dance floor with our first song."

Perfect. Distract him.

Hoisting my purse strap over my shoulder, I yank Aiden by the hand. "Come on."

Aiden almost topples over from the force of my pull on his hand. "What? Are you fucking serious?"

"Totally."

"But you don't even know what they're going to play."

"I don't care."

With Aiden's hand tight in mine, I lead him to the small wooden dance floor. We stand facing each other, both staring at each other helplessly.

Good job, Bea. You started this. Now what?

Taking a step to me, Aiden clasps his right arm around my waist and takes my hand. "Okay, Buzzy. Show me what you've got."

The sounds of a keyboard fill the air. The singer begins to sing something slow. Aiden begins to shift with me slowly in place. "Good song."

After a few lines, a female voice joins in. Aiden holds me closer. "Do you know it?"

"No."

He grins wickedly.

"Just wait."

Suddenly, the music picks up and the singers begin to call each other names like "bum," "punk," and "scumbag," my mouth dropping in shock as they sing even worse expletives.

Aiden laughs heartily at my reaction. "It's called 'Fairytale of New York' by the Pogues and Kirsty McColl, rest her soul."

"Thus the mention of the NYPD," I note.

"Exactly. The perfect Christmas song."

"So you did know it."

"It's the Pogues. I'm Irish. Of course I did."

"Then you're a big liar."

"Not about everything, Buzzy."

And then I realize where I'm standing and with whom. The warmth of Aiden's chest permeates the entire front of my body. His arm is strong around me, protecting me. When I glance up at him, his eyes fix on me, not wavering.

We don't even notice as the song ends. The band quickly starts up again, this time a slow song. I start to pull away, but Aiden's hold on me remains firm.

"Dance with me, Buzzy," he rasps, his warm breath brushing my face.

We dance in place, barely moving. He begins to sing along with the band, whispering the words in my ear.

"What's this one called?" I ask.

"'Irish Heartbeat' by the one and only Van Morrison."

"I like it."

"I'm glad." I can hear the smile in his voice.

Aiden takes our clasped hands and brings them to his chest as I lean closer, shutting my eyes, his male scent of laundered cotton and sweat intoxicating me.

Enjoy this moment. Remember everything.

The song begins to wind down, Aiden holding me even tighter now, to the point where I almost can't breathe, but I'm impervious to it all except for him.

His face inches closer to me, his lips a mere brush away from mine.

Moisture begins to gather in my eyes. I force myself to lean away from him. "I can't."

The band starts to play a fast song, giving me the impetus to pull away from Aiden. I elbow my way back to the table, grabbing my coat and rushing as fast as I can out the door.

Cold winter air punches me in the face as I hurriedly pull on my coat, then grab my phone from my purse. I swipe for the Uber app.

A strong grip encircles my right upper arm. "Bea, stop! What the fuck is going on? Something happened back there and we have to talk about it."

I try to shake him off to no avail while typing in my destination and confirming the ride. "Nothing happened, so there's nothing to talk about."

Suddenly, he turns me around, grabbing me by my shoulders. "That's bullshit and you know it. Will you fucking look at me?"

I bite down hard on my lower lip to prevent the tears that I know are seconds from spilling down my face. I look up just as a sedan with the Uber sign in the front window appears at the curb.

"Please don't go. I'll drive you home," he pleads with me.

"Goodnight, Aiden," is all I can manage as I rush to the car, slamming the door hard behind me. I allow myself one look out the window at the sidewalk where Aiden is standing, his hands at his sides, mouthing my name.

The driver greets me, reciting my address just to confirm the destination.

I nod silently in reply. Rummaging around in my purse, I pull out my phone once more and begin to type furiously in the Notes app, wiping back my tears with the back of my hand.

"THE CONFESSION"

I present myself to you completely naked. You are sitting in a desk chair, wearing nothing but a pair of faded jeans. Your eyes are dark with hunger and lust, your jaw clenched, your lips tightly drawn together. Your arms grip the armrests tightly, as if you're resisting every urge to jump out of the chair and take me right there.

"Kneel," you command me.

I slowly step toward you and settle on the floor in front of you. My heels dig into my backside. I rest my hands flat on my thighs and I bow my head.

"Confess, baby," your voice, low and rumbling, orders me.

I swallow, gathering saliva because my mouth has gone dry.

"For as long as I can remember, I've been told who to be—what to wear, how to speak, what to eat, where to go to school, who I could have as friends. I'm not exaggerating when I call myself the good girl who never misbehaved because I never did. I never got the sex talk from my parents. I learned about sex from books, TV, and movies, not even from my friends. I only had my first real kiss when I was seventeen. He was a groomsman at my cousin's wedding where I was a bridesmaid. What can I say—I was a late bloomer."

I take a long breath and continue.

"College was when I really first started exploring my sexuality. But I was still learning. My first time was with a friend of a friend and it sucked. So painful. I hated it. I didn't understand what the big deal was. Then I met a guy at a mixer and we dated on and off for four years. One night senior year, he drove up to my dorm and I gave him a blow job. I had no idea what I was doing. Once he finger-fucked me in my dorm room, and he told me he was pleasuring me, and it did nothing for me."

I sigh. "Anyway, from that point on, after college, my sex life was pretty tame. I can count on one hand the number of men I've had sex with. Pretty sad, right?"

I swallow again.

"Now I realize what I wanted all along was you. You who always took pleasure in arguing with me, teasing me. It was the equivalent of having a boy pull a girl's braid in the schoolyard, that bizarre notion which supposedly means that he likes her."

I smile slightly to myself.

"And then I saw the real you. How hard you work, the pride you take in your company and the buildings you build. I never knew this about you. It was a revelation for me."

"When we danced together, I felt so safe, so protected in your arms. The way you looked at me turned my pussy so wet. I saw the lust in your eyes, and I don't know if you saw the same mirrored in mine, but I want you to know I wanted you as much as you wanted me."

"Ever since I started writing out my fantasies, I now own my sexuality. I've always known I was a passionate person, and I always thought I'd be good at sex, but never had the chance to explore that... until now. With you."

"I pleasure myself several times a day, and I always do it thinking of you. It's the only outlet I have now."

"So, what am I confessing to? Something I would never imagine

about myself. I love sex. I crave it. I love having a man's cock inside me. And I want yours because I desire it, more than I ever thought possible."

I pause. "This is my confession."

I feel your hand on the top of my head, stroking my hair. "Good girl. That's what I wanted. You, baby. More of you. Do you want my cock now? Or shall I spank you as a reward for your confession?"

"Do as you wish, Sir," I reply quietly. "I'm yours to command."

I hear a rumble in your throat right before you speak again. "I'm going to give you my cock twice. First for my pleasure, then for yours in that tight, gorgeous pussy of yours. Now take my cock into your mouth, baby. I want you to suck me good."

"Yes, Sir," I reply obediently.

I run my hand over your crotch, admiring the bulge in your jeans. I slowly unzip you, gently taking your engorged shaft into my hands, caressing it. I descend with my mouth and give that long vein one sweeping wet lick. I round the crown with my tongue, glancing up quickly at you from below. Your eyes burn as you look at me, your jaw clenched.

Then I swallow you whole, sucking you, working you, taking you as deep as I can until I hit the back of my throat, breathing steadily through my nose. Your masculine, musky smell intoxicates me. I caress your sac, massaging it as I continue sucking you hard, your hands fisting my hair. I can hear you groaning and I feel your muscles lock, your grasp on my hair tightening. You let out a low growl as your warm cum spills into my mouth and down my throat. I swallow as much as I can until it trickles down my mouth and over my chin, then down my chest onto my breasts.

I fall back onto my heels, looking down at my chest. You stroke my hair with your hands. "Beautiful," your voice rasps. You hold out your hand to me to help me up. "On the bed, baby."

I do as I'm told, quickly wiping my mouth with the back of my hand. I lie down and spread my legs, my pussy soaked with desire.

I collapse onto the cool sheets. I fist the cotton between my hands, waiting, craving that first thrust.

You brush the tip of your cock against my folds. "This is what you want, isn't it?"

"Yes," I reply breathlessly.

"Because you're a slut. You're my slut."

"Because I'm your slut," I whisper.

"Again," you command. "Louder."

"I'm your slut."

"You are a slut. Look at you. My cum all over your tits. Your pussy glistening in the light. Your clit swollen with need. Only I do this to you."

"Yes, Sir. Only you. I want only you."

"Good girl," you growl right before you slam your cock into me. "So fucking tight, baby. Tight as a fucking drum. Milk it, slut. Hard."

You grab my hips, your fingers pressing hard into my soft flesh to the point of pain, but I'm completely impervious, reveling in the feel of having you inside me. I press my muscles down hard onto your shaft. My toes curl into the sheet. You pummel me again and again, our moans and grunts combining into a symphony of ecstasy.

I'm riding the most beautiful wave, about to crest and spill over. My muscles lock and I shout in glorious release. I use my Kegels and press down on your engorged cock and milk it with all the strength I have. Your hands vibrate against my hips as you spill into me until every last drop is spent.

You collapse next to me, both of us panting for breath. Once our breathing regulates, you pull me into your side, and I entwine my arms around you.

"That was me. The real me," I whisper.

You tilt my chin so you can look into my eyes. Your eyes bore into me, so warm and molten. "Thank you, baby," you reply, your warm breath wafting over my face.

You bring me closer and place your mouth over mine as we kiss long and deep, not hurried but relaxed. Once we pull apart, we rest together, sated and content. "Such a good girl," you whisper into my hair.

I shut my eyes, smiling to myself because you finally know me, the real me.

7

AIDEN

I punch my pillow a few more times, but it's useless.

I slept like shit. The look on Bea's face when the car pulled away haunted me, keeping me awake most of the night.

And what the fuck did her question about being trapped mean?

I turn on my phone to check the time. 5:03 AM. Motherfucker. I have to be up in an hour.

Before I shut off my phone to try to get at least an hour's worth of decent sleep, I quickly scroll through my emails. One immediately catches my attention.

1028ogirl has a new post.

I touch on the link, and I begin to read the latest prose from Bea. My Buzzy.

I grip my phone so tightly that the metal bites into my palm.

Holy shit. She's writing about me.

I drop the phone at my side, my head falling back on my pillow.

I fucking knew it. The chemistry between us isn't fake. It's real.

She wants me. Beatrice Parker, the Park Avenue Princess, wants me, Aiden Dwyer, the construction worker from Queens.

I yank back the covers, jumping to my feet.

I'm coming for you, baby. Nothing will keep us apart now.

I rush down the hallway to the bathroom.

"Aiden!" my father calls.

"Not now, Pop. I have to go see Beatrice," I yell over my shoulder.

"Son, please," he pleads.

The concern in his voice stops me. When I turn around to face him, he's carrying a copy of today's *New York Post*, his face looking as distraught as his voice sounded.

"What's wrong?"

"Go to *Page Six*."

I snatch the paper from his outstretched hand, turning the pages furiously until I get to the gossip column. The headline reads, "Park Avenue Princess Seen About Town with Hedge Fund Heir."

I swear my heart plummets into my stomach like a fucking boulder.

I quickly scan the report.

"Beatrice Parker, our favorite Park Avenue Princess, granddaughter of *Park* magazine founder Hamish Parker, was recently spotted enjoying the company of Porter Thorne, a scientist at MIT and the son of hedge fund king Gregory Thorne and his socialite wife, Meredith. Not exactly a match we were expecting, but money dates money, especially on the Upper East Side. We're keeping an eye on this pair."

This is bullshit.

My father places his hand on my shoulder. "I'm so sorry."

I shove the paper back at him. "There's nothing to be sorry for because this isn't happening."

"But, Aiden..."

"But nothing, Pop. There's no fucking way she's dating some rich boy geek. This has her parents written all over it."

"How do you know?"

My mind flashes back to Flanagan's last night.

"Have you ever felt trapped?"

"Because I just do. Tell Joe I'll be late today, will ya?"

My father simply nods as I hurry into the bathroom and turn on the shower, washing myself as quickly as I can.

Trapped, my ass.

I've got you, Buzzy. I'm coming.

❀ 8 ❀

BEA

I can hear my parents' voices shouting in the kitchen all the way down from my bedroom.

"Phillip, how did this get into *Page Six*?"

"Because I had *Park*'s publicist call them. I thought it would be best to be proactive in case the media found out about the bailout."

"But *Page Six*? It's so...common."

"Oh, for goodness sakes, Margot! They're the ones who dubbed her the 'Park Avenue Princess.' I didn't see the harm."

I sigh in exasperation, standing at my window, staring out at the view of Central Park.

I haven't been seen in public more than once with Porter since he doesn't even live here.

But I have been seen with Aiden. Nobody would believe that in a million years. The Park Avenue Princess spotted across the river in Queens, and at a construction site and an Irish pub, no less.

Aiden. Dancing in his arms. Our almost kiss.

I lean my forehead against the window, the glass cooling my warm skin.

And now everyone thinks I'm dating some guy I'm not even attracted to. And in the end, I'll have to marry a man I barely know because that's how things are done in my family.

My cell rings, snapping me out of my thoughts. I grab the phone from my nightstand. Marisol's name appears on the caller ID.

"Hey. How—?"

"What in the absolute fuck is going on with you? Did you have a lobotomy I didn't know about? *Chica*, there you were in my house telling me how much you couldn't stand those shit-for-brains society guys and now I open up *Page Six* and you're dating one?" she yells.

I pinch my nose to calm myself and gather my thoughts, knowing she's completely right.

"It's complicated, Mari," I mutter into the phone.

"It's not complicated, Bea. Why do I have the feeling your family is behind all this?"

Because they are. And that's why she's my best friend.

I hear her take a sip of something. "Okay, I'm calm now. I'm here. Tell me what happened."

"In a nutshell, our magazine is losing money. We need an influx of cash and Porter's family is going to invest in it, but our families think that it would look better if he and I started dating in the public eye. Because when this goes public, it won't look as bad if Porter and I are married."

Nothing but silence echoes from Marisol's end. And then a string of Spanish mixed with French. I manage to catch *"loca"* and *"merde."*

She catches her breath. "I swear to God, you stupid WASPs. Sometimes I just can't understand your fucked-up perceptions of what life is supposed to be like."

I imagine her shaking her head at me. "I know."

She clears her throat. "Tell me something, *chère*. Doesn't what you just said to me sound absolutely ridiculous?"

"Yes. Of course," I admit.

"Then why are you doing this?"

"It's my family, Marisol. I can't let them down."

"But you're an adult, Beatriz. You are allowed to say no."

She doesn't understand. "Not when it comes to family. I've been going around and around trying to figure this out, and I haven't come up with much else."

"Have you tried every possible option?" Marisol asks.

"Yes, but I'm not sure it would work. It's a big ask."

"What is it?"

I bite my lower lip. "Maybe you'd want to invest in the magazine so I don't have to marry Porter Thorne?"

She pauses. "Oh wow. I wasn't expecting that."

"I know, but—"

"Stop. It's okay, *chica*. Let's get together and talk about it, especially if it means saving you from marrying that geek."

"He's not really a geek."

She sighs audibly. "Whatever. Look, as batshit crazy as this entire situation is, I'll support you no matter what. If you need to talk to someone, I'm here for you, 24/7/365."

"*Gracias*, sweetie."

"*De nada*. I'll talk to my parents about it and we can have lunch once I do. Love you."

"I will. Love you too."

I end our call, falling back onto my bed in exhaustion.

I turn my head curiously when my parents' voices cease yelling in the kitchen. I jump in place when a loud knock thunders against my bedroom door.

Fuck me. What now...

I rush for the door and yank it open. A pair of angry blue eyes sear into me.

Aiden.

"Porter Thorne? Seriously? That's the name of a James Bond villain!" he growls.

This is not happening.

I pull him into the room, slamming the door firmly behind him. "What the hell are you doing here? And how did my parents not see you?"

He exhales a deep breath, his eyes softening. "They were too busy yelling at each other to notice. But never mind that."

My heart starts to race as his eyes bore into mine.

"Last night. Your question about feeling trapped. That's what this was all about, right?"

I take in his appearance, dressed the same as he was at the building site yesterday—bulky jacket, jeans, and work boots. His face is covered in scruff, probably because he was so intent on seeing me this morning that he didn't have time to shave. But he did have time to shower because I can detect body wash smelling of fresh linen emanating from his skin. And I want nothing more than to kiss him and let him run his lips over me, the sensation of his scruff all over my flesh.

But when he takes me by the shoulders, I remember where I am, who I am, and which family I belong to.

I take a step back. "Yes. Everything's been arranged."

Aiden's eyebrows furrow in confusion. "'Arranged'? What the fuck does that mean?"

I sigh, knowing I have to tell him the truth. "The magazine is losing money, so it's being bailed out by a family who we've known for a long time, and we're going to date for a short period of time. The marriage is just for appearances. You wouldn't understand."

Suddenly, Aiden's eyes turn dark and angry, his fists clenched in fury. "Why? Because I wasn't born with a silver fucking spoon in my mouth? You're damn right I don't understand! You know why? Because that makes no fucking sense. This is your life, Bea. You have a right to live it the way you want."

First, Marisol. Now, Aiden. Tell me something I don't know.

I shake my head, shutting my eyes to keep the forming tears from falling down my face. I can't even look at him. "No, I don't. This is my family. I have no choice."

Without warning, Aiden steps closer to me, taking me by the shoulders. "You have a choice, Buzzy. And that choice is me. I know I'm not what your parents want for you. I live in Queens, I'm not rich, and I have dirt under my fingernails. And it's definitely complicated because your brother is my best friend. But I know you. I know your favorite drink, I know you hate spinach, I know you like to go to Serendipity during the holidays with Seb because it's tradition. And despite the way we've been with each other all these years, throwing insults and barbs back and forth like some fucked-up verbal tennis match, I know you care for me. Last night proved it. I want you, and I know you want me."

I stare helplessly into his eyes, now softer and mirrored with concern.

I do want you, Aiden. More than you'll ever know.

"Even if that were true," I manage, despite my heart catching in my throat, "I have to do this for my family and our reputation. Our society circle—"

His strong hands fall from my shoulders, his eyes fiery again. "Don't even start with the family image excuse," he hisses. "That is bullshit and you know it."

I take a deep breath. "No, it's not, Aiden. My family has a reputation to uphold, and we can't lose the magazine. We need the Thorne money. That's the reality."

I glare at him as he stays silent.

Good. He finally gets it.

Before I know what's happening, he takes my face in his hands, clamping his mouth over mine. My eyes widen from the shock, my hands gripping his shoulders to steady myself from the force of his lips taking mine.

I don't hesitate. My mouth opens to accept his hot tongue. We kiss each other hard and deep, nothing soft or gentle. Quick breaths exhale from our noses. My whimpers and his grunts echo off the walls in my bedroom. I fist his jacket, desperate to take him deeper, further. His hands travel down my back, holding me tighter against him.

Oh God, I want him. I want him so much.

But I can't...

I push as hard as I can against his broad shoulders, releasing my mouth from his. "That will never happen again," I declare determinedly.

He grins slyly back at me. "Fuck yes, it will."

With that pronouncement, Aiden walks past me and exits my room.

My head is spinning. I sink onto my bed, my hand over my heart as if I could stop it from racing.

Once I catch my breath, I spot my laptop on my desk. A rush of endorphins spurs me to my feet. I grab the computer and jump on my bed, clicking on the open link for Prose and begin writing. I know I can't have Aiden, but I need to put these thoughts somewhere. Hopefully, GalwayPlayer will appreciate them.

"QUID PRO QUO"

I stare out at the sea of cars in front of us, red lights lighting up the dark with each start and stop of the vehicles ahead.

I let out a huge yawn. "I hate the BQE," I murmur under my breath. "I hate traffic."

"Anything else?" you ask, and I can't help but laugh at your attempt to rouse me out of my moody state.

I give you a quick list. "Spinach, snakes, and smartass Irishmen."

You tighten your grip on our entwined hands that rest on my left thigh. "Duly noted."

I smile widely to myself and glance over at you. I release my hand from yours so I can rub the back of your head, but you quickly snatch it back and place it on your right thigh.

"I think we might be here a while," you observe, putting the truck's gear into park and switching off the engine, following the example of others in the lanes next to ours.

I sigh audibly, exasperated, my head lolling back in my seat.

Suddenly, I can feel you tugging my hand toward your crotch. "I know a way we can kill time."

My mouth drops. "Are you serious?"

You give me a look that does not welcome debate.

Still very buzzed from the wine we had at dinner, I purse my lips together. “May I ask something first, Sir?”

“Of course, baby.”

“Would you consider a mutual arrangement? A sexual quid pro quo, if you will.”

“Go on.”

I give you a sly smile, then I lift my backside so I can pull up my black Calvin Klein dress. I shimmy it up, giving you a quick glance, but I needn't have wondered if you're in agreement with my suggestion because your eyes are riveted by what I'm doing. I lift myself one more time and pull off my black lace thong, swinging it around my finger.

You grab it from me and shove it into the pocket of your trousers. “I think I'll keep that, thank you very much. Now, lean back,” *you command me huskily.*

I quickly pull up the hem of my dress as far as it can go, then spread my legs open for your access. “I'm already wet, Sir.”

“Good girl. Now, rub your tits while I finger-fuck that sweet pussy of yours.”

“Yes, Sir.”

I do as I'm told. I lean back and begin to rub my breasts through my dress, kneading them until my nipples appear.

You begin rubbing my folds, spreading my essence around them.

“Lovely, baby. Always so wet for me,” *I hear you rasp.*

“It's all you, Sir,” *I whisper.* “Only you do that to me.”

Finally, you insert a finger into me and begin thrusting in and out of my pussy, and then when you add a second, I clench my muscles down hard on them as I dig my Louboutins into the floorboard of the truck, curling my toes inside the snug leather.

I throw my arms over my head, gripping the headrest, my body writhing in my seat. I turn my head toward you so you can see me, the look of ecstasy vivid across my face. The sound of my sucking flesh as you finger-fuck me enraptures me. It is pure audible pleasure for my ears.

And then you press the heel of your hand into my mound, developing a syncopated rhythm with your fingers.

I start to jerk my hips forward in time with you to meet each thrust of your fingers, your hand angling against my clit so perfectly.

I'm so close, riding such a wave of pleasure, sending me soaring until I shout out your name, soaking your hand with my cream.

My heart is racing, my breath panting.

You remove your fingers from my soaked pussy, pressing them to my lips. I take them wholly into my mouth with both hands, sucking on them as I bore my softened eyes into yours.

"Beautiful," you whisper in a rasp.

I glance down at your trousers, now tented by your bulging erection.

I pull your fingers from my mouth with a pop. "Quid pro quo, Sir."

You give me a knowing smirk as I unbuckle my seat belt and lean over the console, giving you a quick deep kiss before placing myself carefully over your thighs. I untuck your shirt from your trousers, nuzzling your muscled abs with my nose, my cheek, luxuriating in their warmth, licking and kissing the entirety of your abdomen, your hand gently caressing the top of my head as I perform my ministrations.

I look at up you, your warm blue eyes searing into mine. Your jaw is clenched. No words are necessary.

I sit up slightly as I slowly begin to unzip your pants. Your cock springs free, hard and begging for my mouth. I give you a quick sly smile and start to lick the crown, sweeping my tongue across the top, licking up the pre-cum that has already gathered, humming my pleasure at the feel of silk over bone in my mouth.

I pull back slightly, then take a deep breath as I swallow you, sliding my mouth up and down your cock, pumping you simultaneously with my hand.

At this angle, your engorged shaft touches the back of my throat as I breathe through my nose.

Your hand fists my hair, wordlessly telling me to go faster. I follow your signal and speed up with my mouth.

Under my chest, I can feel your muscles begin to lock. Your grunts fill the interior of the car, arousing me to my core, knowing I can do this to you, for you.

A loud growl releases from you as you explode into my mouth. I swallow as much as I can, but some of your cum escapes, trickling down my chin.

"Such a good girl," you tell me, running your fingers through my hair.

"Always, Sir. Thank you. I aim to please. Give me a sec."

I lean back and reach for my purse, grabbing a pack of tissues so I can clean us up. I wipe us off, then look up at you and envelop your face with my hands, placing a soft kiss on your lips.

"I enjoyed that," I inform you.

"Likewise," you reply.

"I have an idea for us."

"Do share."

"Car sex."

Your eyes widen in surprise. "Very naughty. But I'd like to point out the obvious that we did just have car sex."

"I know, Sir, but that was oral. It still counts, of course, but I meant vaginal. You up for it?"

You raise your eyebrow at me with your stupidest-question-ever look that I've become accustomed to by now.

I shake my head and smile. "Right. Silly me. It's just that I never did it in a car."

"Yes, privacy partitions can only hide so much in a limousine."

"Ha ha. Very true. Which is why I'm making up for it now."

You grin back at me. "I'm glad I could be of assistance."

"Any specific place in mind?"

You smile wickedly at me. "I have a few."

Suddenly, car engines around us come to life. You lean in and kiss me. "Buckle up, baby."

I give you a wide smile. “Yes, Sir.” I get back in my seat and lock myself into place.

You start the car again. I look out at the sea of cars, now starting to advance forward.

I look down when I feel your right hand take my left, placing it on your right thigh, where it remains for the rest of the drive home.

AIDEN

I take another swig of my beer while I wait for Seb to arrive at our favorite dive bar in the East Village where the drinks are cheap and the jukebox only plays classic rock.

I reread Seb's text on my phone. *Need to talk ASAP. Can you meet me at the Crown Lounge?*

He's never sent an ASAP text to me before, so I knew something was wrong. I got in my truck and crossed the river into Manhattan from Long Island City.

The young prince saunters in, letting in the daylight, making my eyes squint.

"Finally! What took your ass so long? Are all of your Brooks Brothers shirts at the cleaners?"

Seb's lips are pressed together, pulling up the stool next to me. "I need a drink, man."

I can tell he's not kidding. I've never seen him so serious before. So despondent.

I signal to the bartender, gesturing toward my glass and holding up two fingers.

Seb leans his elbows on the bar, running his hands roughly

over his face. "I got the speech, Aiden. The 'Your Playboy Days Are Over and It's Time to Grow Up Because You're a Parker' speech from my dad."

Two tall pints are placed in front of us, froth still spilling down the sides of the glasses.

I watch as Seb takes a long sip of his drink. "You knew it was coming. What brought it on? Bea's forthcoming engagement?"

Seb puts down his glass. "Yeah, and thanks a lot by the way for not telling me the second you heard about that happening."

"How the hell was I supposed to know your family didn't keep you in the loop? Christ, rumors about them are all over social media." I pause before asking my next question. "How is Bea doing?"

"Fuck if I know. She's so quiet. She's not talking to anyone, not even me. It's like she's resigned herself to it and accepted her fate. Porter Thorne, that geek. Of all people. I remember him."

"Is he a bad person?" I ask nonchalantly, just to get any information I can out of him.

"Nah. He's all right. We've known his family for a long time. Friends by default, I guess. But I hate that they're doing this to her. It really kills me."

I know exactly how you feel, brother.

I've texted Bea every day since our kiss in her bedroom, something flirty just so she knows I'm not giving up on her: *Thinking about you, I can't wait for a repeat of that kiss.* But she's ignored my texts, every single one.

I might have to change my strategy.

Seb takes another long draw of his drink. "Let's talk about something else. Oh, hey, I meant to ask you. On New Year's Eve, there's a benefit at the Waldorf, forget what it's for.

Anyway, my family bought a table for it, and I need you there as my wingman."

I shake my head. I know from experience what it's like to be Seb's wingman—having to make small talk with the girl's best friend while Seb plays the one he's interested in, all the while ensuring he doesn't get drunk off his ass and make a total fool of himself.

"No, thanks. I think I'll pass."

"Shit, man. Bea's on the planning committee for it, and—"

Oh, fuck. That's right. The thought of her all dressed up in a sexy dress and fuck-me stilettos...and there's my new strategy.

"Yeah, okay. Why not? Next round's on me," I declare, a huge smile plastered across my face.

"WHAT ARE YOU WATCHING?"

I look up at my father from the leather recliner in front of the TV. I can barely move, thanks to the beers I had with Seb, then dealing with a surprise OSHA inspection at the site, grateful that I got a huge coffee from Dunkin' to sober up before I got back in my truck. It was a shit day all around. I nuked a frozen pizza for dinner because that was all I could handle.

"*The Departed*," I mumble under my breath.

He settles down into the matching recliner next to me. "Excellent."

Just as the Dropkick Murphys begin to launch into "I'm Shipping Up to Boston" during the opening credits, I check the Prose app on my phone. A green dot appears next to 10280girl's profile.

She's online.

I mutter an excited "Yes!" under my breath, jumping up from the recliner.

"Where you going?" Pop asks me curiously.

"Be right back," I shout over my shoulder.

I rush up to my room and sit down at my desk, powering on my laptop and clicking for the Prose website.

My heart pounding, I sign in and immediately click the IM link on her profile.

"Hey 10280girl. I've been thinking about you. I enjoyed 'The Confession' and 'Quid Pro Quo.' You totally aroused me. And I think it's perfectly fine for you not to have had so many lovers."

Come on, Buzzy.

A few seconds, a full minute…and then the bubbles appear and I fist-pump the air. Only two words appear in the message box. ***"You do?"***

I lean back in my chair.

So sweet. Oh God, you're killing me, baby.

GalwayPlayer: "Of course I do. I'm glad you had the courage to open up about yourself."

10280girl: "Thank you. So, I'm guessing from your name that you're Irish. Your family is from Galway?"

Cork, actually.

GalwayPlayer: "Yes."

10280girl: "So, the player part. Does that mean you play a sport or that you date a lot of women?"

I laugh out loud to myself.

No, Buzzy, you're the only woman I want to date.

GalwayPlayer: "I play rugby. And I don't date a lot of women."

10280girl: "Really? No luck, not even with that famous Irish charm?"

Fuck, I wish I could spank you so hard right now.

GalwayPlayer: "I'm very selective."

1028ogirl: **"Got it. LOL. What do you do for a living?"**

Shit! I never thought of an answer for that one.

Think...

GalwayPlayer: **"I'm a high school English teacher."**

1028ogirl: **"Where?"**

Damn it.

GalwayPlayer: **"On Long Island."**

1028ogirl: **"That's so nice. Who are your favorite writers?"**

I exhale in relief. Finally, something I don't have to make up.

GalwayPlayer: **"Steinbeck. Beckett. Flannery O'Connor. Let me guess. You're a Jane Austen fan?"**

1028ogirl: **"I am, but lately, I've been more into the Brontë sisters and their brooders. You know, Heathcliff and Mr. Rochester."**

I grin widely. Why am I not surprised, Buzzy?

GalwayPlayer: **"So, you like them dark and complicated?"**

1028ogirl: **"Hmmm, more like complex."**

Good answer, baby.

GalwayPlayer: **"Judging from your posts, I'm not surprised. I want to ask you a question."**

1028ogirl: **"Okay."**

GalwayPlayer: **"Is there someone specific you're writing about in your posts or just a generalization?"**

I sit back in my chair.

Talk to me, Buzzy. Tell me.

Finally...

1028ogirl: **"I write about someone I have a crush on, but we can never be together. Is that okay?"**

No, of course it isn't fucking okay, because we are going to be together. I want you, Bea.

I shake my head to clear my thoughts.

GalwayPlayer: "It's fine. I'm not offended. You can talk to me. Why can't you be together?"

1028ogirl: "Circumstances beyond my control."

I clench my fists. *Fucking bullshit.*

GalwayPlayer: "So this is why you come here? To meet someone without any strings attached?"

1028ogirl: "I suppose. But honestly, it's just an outlet for me to express my true self."

GalwayPlayer: "And you can't do that otherwise?"

1028ogirl: "Not really. Everyone expects things from me."

GalwayPlayer: "Everyone, meaning family?"

1028ogirl: "Yes."

"Fuck this," I hiss under my breath.

For fuck's sake, you're a grown woman, Bea. You don't have to do everything your family asks of you.

I take a deep breath before I start typing again.

Don't be a shit to her. She needs a friend.

GalwayPlayer: "You don't have to go into details, but just know you can be yourself with me. I'm a good listener."

1028ogirl: "Really?"

I can picture her right now, sitting in her bedroom on Park Avenue, tears forming in her shining green eyes, touched that a stranger, a man she's never met before, would be so selfless with her and not ask for anything in return.

GalwayPlayer: "Really. I mean it."

1028ogirl: "Okay. Look, I hate to do this, but I have to go."

GalwayPlayer: "Just one more question before you go."

1028ogirl: "Yes?"

GalwayPlayer: "Would you like to go exclusive on here so only we can see each other's posts?"

A minute passes, but it feels longer.

Take a chance. Please, baby.

Bubbles appear. She's replying.

1028ogirl: "I'd like that."

"Yes!" I shout out to the air.

GalwayPlayer: "Thank you, 1028ogirl. You've made my night."

1028ogirl: "I'm pleased to know that. Enjoy your evening. We'll talk again soon."

Bet your sweet, lovely, heart-shaped ass we will.

A sharp pain throbs on the left side of my head. A cacophony of sounds assaults me inside the cavernous space of the ballroom at the Waldorf, ranging from the clinking of crystal glasses, the incessant stream of conversation around me, and the thirty-two-piece orchestra on stage belting out a Cole Porter classic.

A female voice behind me shouts above the din, "Have you seen these tacky New Year's Eve decorations? This is the Waldorf, not Times Square!"

I turn around to see who said that. I take a step forward to confront her, but Marisol jumps to her feet, holding me back by the wrist. "Let it go, *chica*!"

I look across at the tables festooned with party favors ranging from hats to horns to celebrate at midnight.

I turn back to my best friend, dressed in a fire-engine-red gown that perfectly accentuates her curves. "It's fucking New Year's Eve! What did she expect?"

"Exactly! So just forget it and enjoy the party."

"I agree, sis."

I turn around to see Seb standing in front of me with a

redhead and a blonde attached to him, his arms lounging casually over their shoulders. But my attention switches to the bowtie hanging around his neck, a large tacky accessory with blinking lights lining its edges.

"Sebastian, what the hell is that?" I ask, pointing at his neck.

"It's New Year's Eve, Bea. I thought it was appropriate for the occasion." He smirks back at me.

"Only you could pull something off like that. You and your bowties."

"It's all in the charm, sister of mine."

"Seb, I'm thirsty," the redhead whines.

"Well, then, we must rectify that situation, shouldn't we?" He steers the women toward the bar, giving me a wave over the blonde's shoulder. "Happy New Year!"

I turn back to Marisol, both of us simultaneously rolling our eyes. "He'll never change," I tell her.

She shakes her head. "I disagree. I bet you the minute he really falls in love, he'll get knocked on his ass, and then he'll really be in trouble."

I laugh at her absurd notion. "Yeah, we'll see."

We sit down again, and I sip some champagne to ease my nerves.

"Is there anything I can do? Do you need anything?" Porter asks me, his clammy hand resting on my bare shoulder.

I completely forgot he was here tonight, and he wasn't helping matters. I accepted that he had a little crush on me, but I didn't realize how serious it was until tonight, constantly checking on me, hovering over me, nervously fiddling with his tie. I know he's just being nice, but every time he's near me, I feel smothered.

"I'm fine, Porter. Really. I just want to make sure tonight goes smoothly."

"Oh yes, yes...of course."

"Just relax."

Before he can reply, a noxious flowery perfume assaults my nose. "Beatrice, darling, what a splendid evening you've created! You've really outdone yourself. The committee is so thrilled with how much we've raised tonight!"

When I turn my head to the right, a chain of diamonds nearly blinds me. Decked out in her finest couture, Penelope Covington gives me a double kiss on my cheeks. I cringe from her close proximity, knowing I'll probably have a sneezing fit any minute.

"It's like a metropolitan winter wonderland in here!" she continues as I nod my head in acknowledgment. "The flowers, the topiaries, the bright lights..."

As she drones on and on, a shiver inexplicably runs up my spine all the way to the back of my neck. The air shifts in the room and everything becomes white noise. The room stills.

Over my shoulder, at one of the exit doors, Aiden is staring right at me.

My breath catches as I take in his appearance.

Dressed in a tuxedo that accentuates his perfectly sculpted body, his dark hair swiped away from his forehead, he is the epitome of a man who exudes confidence and knows what he wants.

And what he wants is me.

Marisol turns her head to see where my attention is fixed. "Holy shit."

At the sight of him, I turn wet from arousal and desire. His face is still covered in scruff. He didn't bother to shave again, which only heightens my hunger for him.

Suddenly he begins to walk toward me, his eyes on nobody else in the room. My heart pounds rapidly inside my chest. As much as I want him, I fear what will happen if I do give myself to him, how many lives would be ruined, how my family's image would be forever tarnished.

I pivot my head away from Aiden, fake laughing at something Penelope says when I sense him standing right behind me.

"Good evening, everyone," his deep voice booms out toward my tablemates.

I laugh nervously. "Oh, Aiden, how lovely to see you. Please allow me to introduce you. Everyone, this is Aiden Dwyer. He and my brother, Sebastian, were at Princeton together."

Delighted smiles and appreciative nods greet him. "Did you row crew there? You look like you could have," one of the older women asks, blatantly flirting with him.

"No, ma'am," he politely replies. "I was too busy keeping Seb out of trouble."

More amused laughs echo around the table, assuming he's joking, but I know better.

Aidan's warm hand sits on my right shoulder. "Forgive me, but I was hoping I could steal Beatrice away for a minute. I have something important to discuss with her."

The hell you do.

"Aiden, have you met Porter Thorne?" I ask, turning to my left, trying desperately to throw off Aiden and his intentions.

Porter jumps from his chair, almost knocking over his water glass. He stretches out his hand to Aiden. "Umm...hi."

"A pleasure. Porter, you wouldn't mind if I had a moment alone with Bea, would you?" he asks, his voice smooth, his stance confident as he towers over Porter.

"No, no, not at all," he answers nervously.

Shit.

"See, Beatrice, he doesn't mind. How about a dance?"

Absolutely not, especially not after how our last dance ended.

Marisol suddenly rises from her chair. "Hey, Porter, let's go dance!" she shouts a bit too enthusiastically.

I don't know whether to hug her or smack her.

She tugs on his sleeve repeatedly until he finally mumbles, "Um...yeah...okay...sure."

I watch Marisol grab his hand, pulling him onto the dance floor.

Aiden's aftershave wafts over me, reminding me he's standing right behind me.

I slap another fake smile on my face. "Forgive me, everyone," I announce. "I'll be back shortly."

"Go ahead, dear. Save a dance for me, handsome," one of the older society ladies replies, giving Aiden a quick wink.

I roll my eyes away from her view, grabbing Aiden's hand, tugging him after me.

"You're kidding me, right? *That's* him?" I hear Aiden shout over the noise. "And where are you taking me? Not that I'm complaining."

"I know this place like the back of my hand," I shout over my shoulder.

I drag him around the corner, away from the ballroom, and into one of the unused coat-check rooms. Testing the doorknob, it gives way. I step in, dragging him with me, locking the door behind us.

I run my hand along the wall, switching on the single light bulb overhead.

I spin around to face Aiden. "What the hell are you doing here?"

He smirks at me. "Seb gave me a ticket."

I shake my head in exasperation. "Of course he did."

"But he's the not the reason I'm here."

I grip the wall behind me, desperate for some form of support. I swallow before repeating my question, a question I already know the answer to. "Then why are you here?"

He steps closer to me, close enough to feel his warm

breath wafting over me. His deep blue eyes pierce mine, unwavering.

My throat goes dry. I lick my lips for some form of moisture. "Damn it, Aiden! Why are you here?" I repeat with a whisper.

He remains mute, his eyes now boring into mine with an intensity that stuns me into silence for a few seconds.

"We can't do this, Aiden. Please," I beg him.

Without warning, he brings his hands to my face, his eyes still on me. He leans in, closer...closer...

His soft, full lips on mine...oh God.

I move my hands from the wall to his broad shoulders to keep myself from falling. The tip of his tongue touches my lips, testing me, asking me for permission.

I open my mouth, silently telling him I want this, I want him.

Slowly, our tongues begin to tangle as my hands move to the back of his head bringing him closer. I want him deeper in me.

I moan from pure desire as I hear him groan from deep within his chest.

Without warning, his mouth pulls away from mine, but only so he can run it along my neck, nuzzling the spot between my neck and shoulder. The scruff on his face tickles my skin. I savor its rough feel on my flesh, humming in pure delight.

"So beautiful, Bea," he murmurs into my ear. "I'm so hard for you."

I tilt my head to the side, allowing him better access. "I want you, Aiden. So much. But not here. And this hotel doesn't book rooms by the hour."

"I know, baby," he pants. "But I need just one taste of you."

I gasp when he squats down to the floor, holding up my

dress with his forearms while pulling down my thong. I glance below to see him staring straight ahead at something.

"What's wrong?"

He looks up at me from the floor, his eyes dark and heavy. "I'm going to fucking devour you, Buzzy."

Before I can reply, he leans in, opening the outer folds of my labia with his tongue and begins to lick my pussy. My head falls back against the wall, slamming into the wood. I'm impervious to the pain because of what Aiden is doing to me. With one hand, I hold up my dress, while running my other one through the tendrils of his dark, thick hair.

A finger inserts itself into me. I take in a breath from the shock. I push his head farther onto my pussy, desperate for him to take in as much of me as he can, grinding myself into his face.

I fist his hair between my fingers. "Oh God, don't stop, please don't stop, Aiden," I plead.

He moans an unintelligible reply into my pussy, inserting one more finger. I start to buck on his face, no longer in control of myself.

I need to come. Fuck, I need to come.

"Yes, Aiden! Right there! Yes!" I scream. With one last shout of his name, I explode in release.

I let go of Aiden's hair and my dress, as he grasps my right hand and kisses the palm. He rises from the floor and roughly takes my face between his hands, kissing me hard and deep. I taste myself on his lips.

When he pulls back, a hardened look appears in his eyes. "Don't run away from me anymore, Bea. We'll figure this shit out. Trust me. Don't freak out about us. Just please don't run."

How can I after that?

I shake my head. "I can't. I won't." I give him a slight smile. "How do I taste?"

He licks his fingers clean, grinning wickedly. "Sweetest thing I've ever had in my mouth."

A loud voice booms the countdown to midnight over the microphone.

Aiden and I lock eyes, counting down together, "Five. Four. Three. Two. One."

"Happy New Year, Buzzy," he whispers to me.

"Happy New Year, Full Ride," I reply.

Our lips meet as we kiss long, soft, wet, and deep. After what seems like hours, we come up for air.

"I want to have you again," he tells me, his voice low and raw.

"When?" I ask breathlessly.

"I'll text you when I know my schedule."

I run my hands over his face. "That's fine. Just don't keep me waiting."

"Never, baby." He pulls a tissue from his pocket. "Here."

I smile, taking it from him, wiping off my mouth. "Thank you. How do I look?"

"Like you just came all over my face."

I roll my eyes at him, smacking his shoulder.

"Well, it's the truth. I just call them like I see them," he replies in defense. "I'm gonna go. Will you be okay?"

My heart drops. "You're leaving?"

His face turns serious. "I think I should. You have a fake boyfriend out there and an image to maintain, remember?"

Back to reality...

I grab him by his lapels, pulling him to me for one more kiss. "Soon, Aiden," I whisper.

"Just try and stop me, Buzzy," he says with a grin, giving me a last quick kiss before turning for the door. He opens it, checking to make sure nobody is outside. He looks back at me, giving me a full smile and a wink before walking out.

I lean back against the wall, my head lolling back, exhaling deeply.

Oh my God...

On shaky feet, I pull my thong back on, then slip out of the small space, closing the door firmly behind me.

I head back to the ballroom. When I reach my table, I frown when I see Porter is back in his seat with Marisol nowhere in sight.

"Where did that lovely friend of yours go, dear?" the same older society woman asks after Aiden.

"He had to leave."

"Oh, that's a shame. Is everything all right, Beatrice? You look quite flushed."

I sit back down in my chair, looking to my left at my soon-to-be fiancé. "I'm fine," I reply to her question, lying not only to her, but also to myself.

◈

Two hours later, I stand at my bedroom window, staring out at the city lights, thinking about the closet, about Aiden, and everything he did to me, everything I felt, everything we said...

His warm tongue on my clit, his rough, callused fingers inside me, pumping me until I exploded, screaming his name.

I'm so aroused. I can't settle down. I need to get this out of me.

I grab my laptop from my desk, lying down on my bed. With my body propped up on my pillows, my fingers fly across the keyboard.

With our legs tangled around each other, I stare into your deep blue eyes, caressing your face with my fingertips.

"Sir, there's something I've been wanting to do for you for a long time now, and I've never done this on any other man because I've never had the desire to do it. No man has ever brought this out in me before."

Your eyes stare back at me in curiosity, then a small grin appears on your face. "How could I say no after hearing a confession like that? What is it?"

"Trust me, it's nothing bad. I promise you'll enjoy it. But I just need you to do one tiny thing for me to fulfill my fantasy, Sir."

"What's that?"

"Lie down."

You get on your back with a wicked smile on your face. I position myself over you, straddling your hips.

"Let me pleasure you, Sir," I whisper. "But may I ask one thing of you?"

"Go on."

"I would like you to not touch me."

"And this will fulfill your fantasy?"

"Yes, Sir."

"Very well. I will do as you ask, but just this one time."

"Thank you, Sir."

I lean in closer over you, giving you a slow, deep kiss.

And then I begin...kissing and sucking you everywhere. I start with your strong chin, then your neck. I take one of your earlobes into my mouth, sucking on it slowly. Your moans fill the air in the room as your hands fist the pillow.

Moving down, I reach your chest. First I tweak your nipples, then I lick them slowly, oh so slowly, sucking on them briefly because I want to get to my destination. The area I've been dreaming about besides the obvious one.

Your abs.

I close my eyes and moan as I move my lips over your hard muscles. I don't lick at first. I brush my lips over them, reveling in their shape, their strength.

And now I can't wait any longer. I extend my tongue and start to lick you everywhere. Everywhere. I can't stop. I grip your hips so I don't miss a single muscle, a single crevice between your pronounced abs.

No man has ever provoked this reaction in me. I can't stop. I moan as I lick you. Your raw, male scent intoxicates me. You groan, making me so wet.

And against my body, your cock presses against me, nudging me, requiring my attention.

Patience. I'm saving that for last. I just need to do this first. To afford us both this pleasure.

Finally, I move farther down your happy trail with my tongue, nuzzling the scatter of dark hair lining the way. I take a brief moment to adjust my position between your legs.

And then, I take your cock into my mouth, first licking your pre-cum off the tip, then swallowing you whole. I pump with my mouth and hand. I hum as I move up and down your engorged shaft.

I can feel your muscles locking, and it doesn't take long until you explode in my mouth.

I wipe my lips with the back of my hand, kissing your inner thighs before I move back up your body, settling in next to you.

"May I touch you now?" you ask.

I nod, and within seconds, your mouth is devouring mine.

"So, my good girl has a few fantasies, I see."

I laugh quietly to myself. "Just a few, Sir."

"Do let me know if there are any others you need fulfilled, baby. I'd be more than happy to help you out with them," you inform me with a wide smile crossing your face.

"Thank you, Sir. I will."

You brush your lips against mine. "Good girl."

I smile back at you. "Always."

I check myself for the hundredth time in the mirror by the front door. Inhaling deeply, I shake my hands to loosen them, but when I clench them again, I find my palms sweaty.

What the fuck is wrong with me?

I'm about to have sex with Beatrice Parker, my best friend's younger sister, the woman I've been lusting after for too many years to count. My Buzzy.

Oh, right. That's why I'm freaking out.

Idiot.

A ping sounds from my phone. Pulling it from the back pocket of my jeans, a text from Bea appears when I swipe it open.

Almost there.

Fuck. I can't remember the last time I've been this nervous. And after reading her latest post on Prose, "The Trail to Happiness," I'm even more anxious, hoping I can give Beatrice what she wants, what she needs.

Speaking of, I meant to reply to her about it. I pull out my phone and swipe the Prose app.

"My 10280girl, you have pleased me enormously with 'The Trail to Happiness.' It aroused me to know you carry such a fantasy inside you. Perhaps one day we can make it a reality."

I notice a green dot on her profile. She must be online now.

Why the hell is she on Prose in the first place? She could have the real thing with me. Is there something else I don't know about her?

I hear a car door slam shut. When I look outside, I see Beatrice in a car with her phone in her hand, probably reading my message. She looks up and quickly shoves it into her purse. Once she's on the sidewalk, she straightens her coat and gives her long, flaxen blond hair one last toss over her shoulder.

Those two simple, innocuous gestures make my cock turn to stone, and I haven't even touched her yet.

I open the door, watching as she grips the bannister, slowly making her way toward me, averting her eyes, but I know she's seen me waiting for her.

Closer...

Closer...

Finally, she reaches the porch and looks up at me, giving me the shyest smile I've ever seen on her face.

It's okay, baby. I'll take good care of you tonight.

"Hi," she greets me softly.

"Hi back," I murmur roughly under my breath, barely able to contain myself.

We stare at each other for what seems like an eternity, and I don't even have to ask her what she's thinking because I know right now, at this very moment, we share the same mindset.

We're going to fuck tonight. Long, hard, and deep.

She coughs slightly, bringing me back to this moment.

My face heats in embarrassment. "Oh, shit. Come in."

I step aside as she enters the house. She puts her purse down on the side table by the door. As she begins to remove her coat, I help her from the back, taking it in my hands to hang it in the hall closet.

When I turn around, my breath is taken away.

She's wearing a tight, black, silk wrap dress, the soft fabric accentuating her perfect curves. Black silk stockings encase her long legs, and the sexiest pair of fuck-me black leather boots reach all the way from her toes to just over her knees.

I can't keep myself from staring. She smiles coyly and steps closer. Her perfume wafts over me, intoxicating me with its spicy, sultry scent.

Bea starts to run her hands over my chest, feeling the fabric of my gray cashmere V-neck sweater. "Very nice," she purrs.

I grin back at her. "You approve?"

"Mmm-hmm. Very much." She bites her bottom lip. "Are we alone?"

"Yes, ma'am. My dad's at Flanagan's for his weekly poker game. He won't be home until much later."

She nods at my reply, flashing me a sexy smile. "Good to know."

I tug her closer to me and clamp my mouth over hers. She swiftly opens for me, accepting my tongue. I clutch her tightly, to the point where we're fucking each other's mouths.

Wordlessly, I pull away and, yanking her by the hand, I tug her with me up the stairs, down the hallway to my bedroom.

Once inside, I shut the door behind me, turning to press her against the hard wood. The curtains are drawn, and the only source of light in the room comes from the lamp on my nightstand.

Okay, not the only one...

Her nose lifts curiously into the air. "What's that smell?"

"Candles," I mumble under my breath.

She rubs her hands over my face, the pads of her fingers soft against my stubble. "Awww, you lit candles just for me?" she coos with a bite of sarcasm. "You're so sweet."

"Not for much longer because I'm going to fuck you so hard you'll be begging me not to stop."

"Promises, promises..." she whispers as her thumbs caress my lips.

She raises her left leg to coil around my waist as I reach under her dress to rip off her panties. But when my hand touches her pussy, it's bare of any fabric.

Oh, fuck yes...

I groan in pleasure from this discovery. Her mouth briefly pulls away from mine. "No bra either," she whispers breathlessly.

My eyes roll behind my closed lids.

"You're killing me, Buzzy," I moan under my breath as I start to rub her folds while nuzzling her neck.

"I don't plan to until after I know what it's like to have you inside me," she purrs in reply.

I laugh under my panting breath. "Fine with me. Speaking of which..."

I don't even know what I want to do to her first. My dick is hard as a fucking rock. But I know what I want first, what I've wanted to know for too long...

I pull back from her, and giving her a sly grin, I untie the knot at the side of her waist. The smile on her face mirrors mine as she leans away from the door, her eyes never leaving mine, dropping her arms to the side, allowing the silk fabric to flutter to the floor.

The only clothes she's left wearing are black silk stockings and her boots.

My mouth falls, but I shut it quickly to stop myself from drooling over her like a pubescent schoolboy.

"You like?" she asks, a sexy glint in her eye.

Her breasts are perfectly round, her areolas a dusty pink contrasting with the light pink of her nipples, pointing straight at me. Her skin is creamy like fresh milk, and I want to lick every inch of it.

I don't answer. I drop to my knees, reaching for her right foot. I run my hands over the soft flesh of her upper thigh, then the supple leather of her boot. One of her hands runs through my hair as I slowly unzip it, the sound echoing off the walls of my bedroom. I lift her leg to remove it, then languorously run my tongue along her inner calf, causing Bea to moan in pleasure above me. I switch to her left leg, affording it the same that I performed on her right.

A flash of red catches my eye from the bottom of the boot. "Red. Very nice."

She smiles widely. "All Louboutins have red soles."

"Lou-who-what now?"

Her amused laugh fills the room, sending me soaring. "Christian Louboutin. He's a French shoe designer. He's a genius."

"Well, then...*Merci, Monsieur Louboutin.*"

Bea puts out a hand to me. "Enough talking, Full Ride."

Smiling to myself, I take her hand to help me up from the floor.

Without warning, she grabs my head and pulls me to her to kiss me again. Her heart pounds against my chest as I'm swept up in her, my hunger for her just as desperate.

"Arms up," she orders in a raspy voice, causing my cock to turn even harder, pushing against the constraints of the rough fabric of my trousers.

I obey her without hesitation, closing my eyes as she pulls my sweater over my head. Her eyes never leave mine when she undoes my belt buckle, then just as rapidly unzips my pants, shoving them down my legs.

I tug Bea into my arms once more while removing my socks using my toes. Placing my hands firmly on her lovely round backside, I pick her up, her legs instantly rounding my waist. My right hand grips the back of her head as we kiss each other hard, tongues tangling. I keep one eye open to gently lay her down on my bed.

Bea lifts her body to push the covers under her to the foot of the bed. I can't help but stop and stare at her lying on my navy cotton sheets, her blond hair spread over the pillows.

This is it. I'm going to make love to my Buzzy.

"I want you, Aiden."

Those four words. I've heard them in my fantasies when I jerked off with her image in my head, and now she's here, saying them to me in my bedroom.

I carefully ease onto the bed, hovering over her.

"Say it again," I command her.

Her emerald eyes warm, turning into molten steel. "I want you, Aiden," she replies obediently.

I carefully lay on top of her, adjusting my weight. She encircles her arms around my shoulders, kissing me so long and deep, but I need more. I need to taste her. To know what her lush tits feel like on my tongue, in my mouth.

I pull my mouth from hers, nuzzling her neck, the space between her neck and shoulders, then begin to chart my course down along her chest, taking my time until I can't hold back.

I stare in awe at her tits waiting impatiently for my mouth, her nipples hard and pointed. I lick one first, kneading it, feeling its weight in my hands. Then I dive in, suckling it, playfully licking the end of the nipple with the tip of my tongue, eliciting moans of "God, yes, baby!" from my Bea.

I switch over to the other breast, awaiting my mouth. I can't help but just dive in, sucking it whole, squeezing the other one with my hand. Bea writhes beneath me, squirming and groaning in pleasure. "Don't stop, Aiden."

Hearing her moan my name sends me into hyper-drive. My cock is engorged to the point of pain. I have to be inside her, to fuck her until she forgets everything except the feel of me.

I trail my tongue down to her belly, close enough for the scent of her desire to intoxicate me. I give her wet pussy one long lick, sending Bea's back arching so completely that I have to hold down her thighs.

"I want your cock inside me, Aiden. Please..." she begs, her voice deep and hoarse with desire.

"Tell me more, Bea. Tell me what you desire most," I order her as I insert a finger into her soaked cunt.

Tell me, baby. You can trust me. Tell me everything.

"I want your cock inside me, fucking me hard and deep until I come and scream your name at the top of my lungs."

Her words paralyze me. I reach over her to my night-stand, giving her tit a quick bite as I grab the open condom packet I left on top.

"Listen to my Park Avenue Princess, such dirty words coming from her sweet innocent mouth," I whisper into her ear before sitting up to slide the rubber onto my shaft. "Tell me what you want, Buzzy. Right now. Say it."

Her eyes stay shut, but I can see them quivering behind her eyelids, her head falling back farther onto the pillow. "Fuck me, Aiden. Please fuck me."

Like a man possessed, I slide back to the foot of the bed, yanking her legs up onto my shoulders. She gasps in surprise, gripping her hands onto my thighs.

I settle onto my knees, sliding my dick into her so seamlessly, like a fucking glove. We simultaneously sigh from surprise and pleasure, luxuriating in the feel of each other.

I glance down at her, a look of pure joy on her face. Knowing I've done that to her, I want, I *need* to give her more.

I start to thrust, then slide out, testing to see how much she can take and how far I can go. I'm sheathed inside her pussy, her cunt tight as a drum on my cock, the most glorious sensation I've ever had.

I can't help myself. I start pummeling her, pounding her, her nails now digging into the back of my thighs, but I don't give a shit. She can leave scars for all I care. I'm finally fucking the love of my life.

The sound of my flesh slapping against hers fills the room. I shut my eyes to savor it. Screams emanate from Bea's mouth. "Yes! Yes! Aiden, don't stop!" And I don't. I only pummel her faster. Her muscles tighten even more around me, and I know she's close.

Her hands fall from my thighs to grab the sheet beneath her, fisting the cotton in her hands. Her head swivels back and forth. "Aiden!" she screams at the top of her lungs.

I watch in awe as her body shudders, riding the wave of her orgasm. Her pussy bears down on my cock, milking it so hard.

I start to shake as I explode, my muscles locking from the power of my release.

Completely spent and fully sated, I let her legs fall from my shoulders, collapsing on top of her, the sweat from my body mixing with the perspiration on her chest.

Our breaths match pant for pant. I shiver as Bea slowly runs her fingernails down my back. Her touch is soft and gentle.

When I finally raise my head to look at her, I can see tears in the corners of her eyes. I wipe them away with the pads of my thumbs, giving her lips a soft kiss.

"Don't be scared, baby. It'll be okay, I promise. I've got you now."

She nods her head silently in reply. I shift myself, taking her warm body into my arms as she lays her head in the crook of my neck.

I've got you, Buzzy. I've got you.

"A WALL AND A PAIR OF PIGALLES"

I feel so sexy. I can't wait to show you.

Here I come...

I step out of the bathroom and walk toward you. All I'm wearing is my black-beaded choker and my Pigalles.

From your place on the sofa, you watch me like a lion about to devour its prey. You're holding a flogger in your hands, slapping the end of it against your palm. Your legs are crossed, an ankle resting on the opposite knee.

"Stop," you command me. I stand in place as your eyes roam over me.

You point to a nearby wall. "Face forward and lean against it with your palms resting flat, and stick that gorgeous ass of yours as far out as it will go. Present yourself to me," you order in a rasp.

My heart pounds furiously inside my chest. My pussy is soaked from your voice alone.

I position myself against the wall as you ordered me, my ass sticking as far out as it will go.

I listen to the footfalls on the floor as you make your way to me. I hear you grunt in approval.

The ends of the flogger travel up and down my back, trailing my spine. I start to shiver, goose bumps rising along my arms.

"So beautiful," you murmur. "Those shoes, baby. You look so fucking hot."

I shut my eyes, absorbing your words, reveling in them.

"I can't decide which to use first. My hand on your ass or the flogger."

No doubt in my mind.

"I want both, Sir. Please," I beg.

"That's my good girl." I know you're pleased because I can sense the smile on your face. God, how I love pleasing you.

Without warning, your hand smacks me twice across my backside. I moan from your ministrations.

You slap me again, this time with the flogger. As much as I love it, I think I love your hand more, because it is your flesh on my flesh.

"I'm going to rub your pussy now with this, but you're not allowed to come. Do you understand?"

"Yes, Sir."

You do just as you say. I hold my inner muscles together. I moan over and over. I need to come so badly, but as tempted as I am to see what would happen if I disobeyed you, I decide to behave.

"Good girl."

I hear the flogger fall to the floor. "How wet are you, baby?"

Your hand travels between my legs, searching out my pussy. Your fingers reach my folds, massaging the wetness more, spreading it all over.

"Very nice," you whisper into my ear, your hot breath breezing through my hair. I smell myself on your fingers as you raise them to my nose. "Lick." I open my mouth and eagerly accept your offering. I suck on them, moaning as I wrap my tongue around your fingers.

"Open."

I open my mouth as you pull out your finger with a pop.

Then your hands travel to my breasts. You take one in each hand, kneading them, and when you move up behind me, and I sense your cock brush against my ass, I shut my eyes. My head falls back onto your chest, moaning with each pull and tweak on my nipples.

"You feel amazing, baby. I bet you want my cock, don't you?"

"Oh God, yes, Sir. I want it so much."

You rub your shaft farther into my ass. "Very soon, baby, I'm going to claim this. And it's going to be amazing for you."

I swallow at the thought of him inside me. "It will be, because I trust you, Sir."

"Good girl. But for now, I'm going to fuck your pussy nice and hard."

I moan. "Yes, please, Sir. Hard and deep."

You ease your cock into me. You don't wait. You begin thrusting into me, gripping my hips. All I can hear in the room are your grunts and my cries of "Yes!" and "Don't stop!"

God, you feel so fucking good inside me. You pound into me so hard, my hands barely hang on to the wall where I press them.

My body begins to shudder and my muscles lock onto your cock as my orgasm overtakes me. I am liquid and boneless as you come soon after.

"Please, Sir, may I remove my hands from the wall?"

"Yes, you may," you rasp under your breath.

I drop my hands from the wall as I fall back onto your body. You grab hold of me as we both sink to the floor together, my sweat-covered body collapsing onto you.

I fall onto my side, my arm stretched across your chest. We're both panting loudly. I look over and you're staring back at me, your eyes blazing.

I can't help myself. I roll closer to you and kiss you long and wet. And before I know it, I'm wet again, and I know you feel it too because you hurl yourself on top of me and slam your cock into me. I lock my ankles around your torso, growing wetter at the thought of what we look like from above, with my Pigalles tangled around your long, lean body. I feel so alive, so sexy, so desired.

My fingernails dig into your flesh as you pummel me. I'm

completely impervious to the burn of the floor on my back. Nothing matters but the feeling of having you inside me, and then we come together, your head rearing with your growl from erupting inside me. My eyes shut from such exquisite release. You fall onto the floor and against my side.

"Oh my God," I whisper. "That was...I can't even put it into words."

"Fucking amazing," you offer.

"Yeah, that works," I reply, letting out a small laugh.

After a few more minutes of panting and waiting for our heart-beats to regulate, you rise to your feet, then pull me up.

"Take off your shoes," you command me.

You offer your hand so I have something to balance on as I step out of one Pigalle, then the other. Once I'm barefoot, you take my hand and lead me toward the bathroom.

"May I ask where we're going, Sir?"

"Shower," you reply over your shoulder.

"But I can barely stand," I counter. "And I think my pussy needs a rest."

"I think you'll both be able to manage it." I can hear the wicked grin in your voice.

Who am I kidding?

Of course I can manage it. Because I'm your good girl. Always.

BEA

Lying on my bed with my phone, I attempt to focus on replying to the emails that I've been ignoring.

Just as I open one, I can't help myself.

I pull up the silk on my nightgown and stare in wonderment at my left breast.

Two bruises mark my skin. One is small and yellow, almost at the top where breast meets bone. The other is more distinct and multicolored, situated to the right of my areola.

I smile to myself. Aiden.

I hadn't even realized they were there until I took a shower this morning and saw them reflected back at me in the mirror when I was drying off.

All I can remember about the moment when Aiden gave me those bites is looking down at him and reveling at seeing him sucking me so intently, not even groaning or moaning, just enjoying my body.

Aiden asked me to give him a chance, but nothing has changed with my family. We still need the infusion of cash for the magazine to survive, which means I'll probably be trapped in a loveless marriage.

But after being with Aiden, I can't let that happen. I need to talk to Marisol.

I check my phone, yet again, to see if I've received a message from GalwayPlayer. I'm anxious to learn what he thinks of my latest vignette.

But Aiden's face flashes in my mind. Am I betraying him by continuing with Prose? We're just having a good time, right? Aiden doesn't really love me. It's only lust, and I'm someone he knows he can't truly have. And if he knew about my fantasies, he'd probably see me as some slut and think less of me. I couldn't bear the thought of that.

Fuck. I have no idea what to do.

My cell rings, jolting me out of my thoughts. Seb's name is on the caller ID. "Hello, brother of mine."

"Hey, sis," he replies roughly.

"Long night?"

"Something like that. I have no idea where I am."

"Well, you're alive, so that's all that matters. What's going on?"

"Why are you marrying Porter Thorne?"

I lean back into my pillows. "Wow, you just come right to the point, don't you? You know why. We need to get the magazine back—"

"Whoa! Pump the brakes! What does *Park* have to do with it?"

"It's losing money, Seb. Didn't you know that? The Thornes are infusing a substantial amount of cash into it, and the marriage is just a cover in case word ever gets out."

Seb goes silent before replying. "What the fuck, Bea? You can't do that. You're marrying that geek just to save the magazine?"

"It's our family legacy, Sebastian. Doesn't that mean anything to you?"

"Shit, why didn't you tell me? And why didn't Mom and Dad tell me about *Park*?"

"I don't know. You'd have to ask them. But just a shot in the dark, maybe it's because you're too busy partying, and they see me as the responsible one, no offense."

"None taken."

"Look, don't worry. I have a plan so maybe I won't have to go through with it. I just have to talk to Marisol and a few other people I trust."

"Umm...yeah. Marisol...yeah," he stammers. "That's a good idea."

My brows furrow at his nervous response. "Seb, what's with you?"

He coughs as if clearing his throat. "Nothing. Just keep me posted. Gotta go."

I stare at my phone, wondering what the hell just happened. Never mind.

Returning to my emails, I scroll through them, answering the important ones and discarding the spam when a message pops up from Prose, *You have a message from GalwayPlayer.*

I quickly open the app, smiling at what I'm reading.

GalwayPlayer: Hi 1028ogirl. I can't stop thinking about your Pigalles. Those shoes sound so sexy.

My entire body warms at his compliment.

1028ogirl: Thank you. I love Louboutins. I know the heels are awful high, but he designs them so they feel comfortable on a woman's foot.

GalwayPlayer: How many pairs do you have?

1028ogirl: Too many to count.

GalwayPlayer: They all have red soles, don't they?

1028ogirl: Yes, they do, actually.

My hands hover over the keyboard. Another image of Aiden flashes into my head, reverting back to his bedroom when he was taking off my boots.

GalwayPlayer: Something wrong?

I shake my head to dissipate the image.

1028ogirl: No, it's nothing. It's weird you asked that because I just had a conversation with my brother's friend about this same topic. Funny, right? lol

I stop typing and wait to see if he's writing back a reply. It's a good minute before finally I see the bubbles.

GalwayPlayer: Shit. I'm sorry, but my boss just came in. Talk soon. Promise.

A caption pops up onscreen next to his name: **GalwayPlayer is no longer online.**

I lean back against my pillows. I quickly reread our exchange, my brows furrowing over why he freaked out on me.

Maybe his boss really did come in, so that could be legit.

I shake my head. What's with the nervous men today?

Fuck!

I'm a lucky son of a bitch. And a stupid one as well. I can't believe how close that was. I almost blew my cover by asking about those fucking shoes of hers.

I lean back in the desk chair, running my hands through my hair.

A brisk knock sounds at my bedroom door. "Come in, Pop."

I glance over to see my father dressed in his pajamas and robe. He sniffs the air. "What is that?"

"Plum orchid," I mutter under my breath.

"Excuse me?"

I clear my throat. "It's the scent of the candles from last night."

He nods. "I see. So while I was losing my pension to Ryan Connelly at Flanagan's last night, you were entertaining a lady friend?"

I laugh. "God bless you, Pop. 'Lady friend.' You're too old school for your own good."

"Well, it fits since last time I checked, I was old. So, who was she?"

"Nobody you know," I reply, praying he stops there with the interrogation.

No such luck.

"So if I don't know her, then you can tell me the young lady's name."

My jaw clenches. "I can't."

I watch as he takes a few steps and sits down on my bed. "Look at me, Aiden."

I turn around in my chair and face my father head-on.

"I wasn't born yesterday," he begins. "The mere fact that you won't tell me who was here last night tells me enough."

I swallow in my throat, waiting for his admonishment to come. But it never does.

"It's your life and I'm not going to judge you for it. But you can't mess with her head. She's probably going to end up with someone else, someone her parents think is suitable for her, probably that guy who was mentioned in the paper."

"But she'll never love him," I counter.

"That may be, but you need to accept—"

"No, I won't!" I insist. "It's all her family's doing. She'll never marry him."

"But has she told you she loves you?"

"No, but—"

He raises his hand to me, palm facing out. "She's a lovely girl, son. I adore her. And I don't want to see her get hurt, and for that matter, I don't want the same for you. Am I clear?"

I purse my lips and nod. "Yes, Pop. I swear, I'll never do anything to hurt her."

"And you also need to think about what this would do to your friendship with Sebastian. Having him as your best friend is one thing, but I'm not sure how dating his sister would go over with him."

I sigh. "Yeah, I know. I need to think about that too."

My father nods, rising to his feet. He pats me on the shoulder and walks out, his words still echoing in my head.

I was wrong. There is one way I can hurt her, and it's by not being truthful with her.

I have to tell her about GalwayPlayer. Soon. But until then...

I sit down at my desk and open the bookmark for Prose, the words flowing from my mind as easily as breathing...

"YES, SIR."

You look up at me from where you're kneeling on the floor. And you know it's time to say it. What I want to hear from you more than anything.

"I submit to you, Sir."

A slight grin appears across my lips, and my eyes instantly grow heated.

"Come to me and lie across my lap, ass facing up."

I can't wait. I know what I'm going to do to you. My cock immediately hardens and I need to come so badly. But I know it'll only happen when I'm inside you, arousing me even more.

You slowly rise to your feet as I ease back farther on the bed. You climb on and stretch across my thighs, your arms reaching out as far as they can go.

My hands roam over the warm flesh of your backside, stroking you slowly.

"Do you submit to me?" I ask roughly.

"Yes, Sir," you whisper.

A loud smack echoes throughout the room as my hand lands on one cheek of your buttocks. Your moans echo off the walls.

"Louder," I command.

"Yes, Sir," you reply, following my order.

I spank you again, and you moan from the exquisite pain I afforded you.

"More, please, Sir," you beg.

I tunnel my hand into you, checking your pussy. You can't help but buck and writhe from my touch.

"Oh, God, please, touch me there, Sir."

"No, not yet, darling. Remember who sets the rules," I remind you.

"You do, Sir," you answer promptly.

"Good girl," I reply, delivering another smack to your ass, then soothing it as I rub my palm over your heated skin.

Without warning, I pull you up and kiss you long and deep. You accept my tongue and suck on it like sweet candy.

I pull away, but my eyes remain focused on yours. "Now, I want you to lie back against the pillows and present yourself to me because I'm going to fuck you."

You scoot back farther onto the bed, pushing yourself until your back hits the pillows. You lie down and spread your legs open, waiting for my command.

"Give me your wrists," I tell you.

You offer them to me willingly, presenting them pressed together, not apart. My heart pounds inside my chest, leaping at your subservience, how open and willing you are, how much you trust me.

You smile so sweetly at me. "I want to experience it all. To know what it's like to give up control, to let someone tell me what to do for a change."

I pull out a silk necktie from the nightstand and begin to bind your wrists. "Wiggle your fingers to make sure the circulation is flowing properly."

You obey me, all ten digits moving freely.

I reach for the black silk eye mask I left on the nightstand. I look at you one last time. Your emerald eyes are heated, no doubt from the look of power and lust emanating from mine.

I give you one last grin, then adjust the mask over your eyes, pushing your arms over your head.

"Do not move. If you do, I'll punish you," I instruct.

"Yes, Sir."

"Good girl."

You shiver from the lack of cover over your body. "Don't worry, baby. You won't be cold for long," I reassure you.

I feel your warm breath on my face. "Can you see me?" I ask.

"No, Sir."

"Are you telling me the truth?"

"Yes, Sir."

With your vision obscured, I smile contentedly. You are pleasing me so well.

I move down your body, I stop, and then....my mouth and hands are on your right breast—licking, sucking, biting, nipping, kneading. I catch a glimpse of your hands clasping together so you have something to hold on to because the pleasure is so intense for you...so over-whelming.

My tongue licks a trail down your stomach, over your rounded belly...I can hear your breath turning rapid...I can tell you want to come, you need to come...but I won't allow it...not yet.

I lick circles on your belly, torturing you to see how much you can take.

"Please, baby," you beg.

"Excuse me?" I ask roughly.

"I'm sorry. Please, Sir," you correct yourself.

I quickly lift your body and deliver a swift smack on your back-side. "Apology accepted. Good girl."

And then once I lay you back down, I move farther south. I devour your folds, kissing them as if I were kissing your mouth.

You moan. "Oh, fuck yes! Fuck yes!"

And then I suck your clit...and you lose your mind, screaming, writhing and squirming despite my arms locked around your thighs, holding you down.

"Please let me come, Sir. Please," you plead.

Oh no, not yet, my good girl.

I insert a finger into your pussy, and then another. You clamp down hard with your Kegels.

"Come for me now, baby!" I shout above your groans and pleas.

I watch as your body shudders and bucks from the orgasm that won't stop. I lick your essence with my tongue like a contented feline lapping cream from a bowl.

I sense your body relaxing. I hear you pant to catch your breath. I pull away from your sweet pussy, a wide smirk on my face as I settle myself next to you. I slowly undo the mask from your face. Your head lolls to my side. I grip your chin.

My voice comes out in a growl. "Taste yourself on me, baby. So amazing."

Your mouth covers mine. I can tell by the need and desire in your eyes that you want to touch me, to wrap your arms around my neck, run your hands through my hair, then hold my head steady so you can kiss me long and deep. But I haven't given you permission to move your hands from above your head. You will have to wait until I allow you that pleasure, that thrill of holding me close.

Your tongue tangles with mine. Your cream mixed with your warm tongue...pure fucking bliss.

I pull my mouth from yours. I raise myself on my elbows to hover over you.

"Do you want it, baby?" I ask you.

"I want anything you allow me to have, Sir," you reply.

"Do you want my cock?"

"Yes, Sir. Please. More than anything."

I slide up your body, your heat enveloping me. The tip of my cock trails over your belly, over your chest, finally lying between your breasts. "Taste it, honey. Show me you want it," I command you.

You lean your head up and stick out your tongue, licking the tip like a lollipop, tasting me in your mouth.

I pull back. "Good girl."

"Always. I'm always your good girl, Sir."

So sweet. So submissive.

I lean down to place a quick yet deep kiss on your lips. You smile because you know you've pleased me.

I move down your body, pulling you by the hips. You know what's coming next. I'm going to fuck you with my cock. You are so wet from the anticipation.

I settle myself, and then slowly I ease into you. We both gasp from the sensation of being joined together. More than anything, I need to move.

"I'm going to fuck you now, baby," I declare.

"Yes, please, Sir."

"Beg me, baby."

"Please fuck me, Sir."

I hear the lust in your voice, arousing me until my cock is engorged. I can't stop myself. I thrust inside you until the need is so overwhelming that I pick up speed, the friction causing sweat to form on my forehead, my back.

I pummel you as your voice calls out to me, "Yes, Sir! Yes, Sir! Don't stop! Fuck me, Sir!"

My fingers dig into the soft flesh of your hips, as I pound into you. The sound of flesh slapping flesh fills the room. My grunts and your screams bounce off the walls.

You feel so fucking amazing sheathed around my cock. I'm riding a wave of fucking ecstasy. And then I move and brush against your clit.

You start to scream "Yes!" and "Right there!" over and over. Your inner muscles tighten around me like a vise, and then you come loudly, screaming in release.

Your sweet pussy milks my cock, and then, with the exquisite release, my entire body shudders, collapsing on top of you.

We both pant for fresh oxygen. You stretch your arms to get the circulation going. I look into your shining eyes, so alive, so vibrant, and you bring your arms around me, holding me.

You lean into me and whisper in my ear, "Thank you, Sir."

I brush the pads of my fingers against your delicate cheek. "That's my good girl."

❧ 14 ☙

BEA

"Ladies, I asked you all here to thank you for your hard work on this year's benefit. We managed to raise..."

I chew thoughtlessly on another breadstick as Penelope Covington drones on about the success of the benefit. Sitting in her sumptuous dining room, I look around at the other committee members whose eyes are fixed on the woman, as if she were sent down by God Himself to preach the gospel to a flock of unwashed heathens. In this case, that's not too far off the mark except all the women at this table are coiffed, groomed, and dressed by the finest salons and boutiques on Madison Avenue.

The table begins to vibrate under me. I look down at my phone sitting next to my right arm.

The screen reveals a text from Aiden.

Sext me. Now.

My eyes nearly pop out of their sockets.

Surely he can't mean....

I gracefully reach for my cell, flashing a fake smile and mouthing "Sorry" to everyone. Marisol raises her brows at me

131

in curiosity. I shake my head at her, mouthing "It's Seb" in return.

Where are you? I ask.

It's no concern of yours. Do as I said.

I can't. In the middle of a ladies' lunch. Later.

I place my phone back on the table, but he texts back just as quickly. Does he not understand the definition of "later"?

Would those ladies be fascinated to know how loudly you scream when you come? How deep and hard the Park Avenue Princess likes to be fucked?

Damn him.

I rub my thighs together, inhaling deeply at the mere thought of what he did to me.

You're wet right now, aren't you?

How does he know?

Yes.

Good girl. Go to the restroom. Now.

I slowly push my chair back and grab my clutch, waving the phone in my hand to indicate that I have a pressing matter, unbeknownst to them it being that my thong is soaked and that I'm about to do something shocking in Penelope Covington's perfectly appointed guest bathroom high above Fifth Avenue. I don't even dare to look at Marisol because she'll just want to know more, and I want to do this before I think it through and propriety wins out over desire and spontaneity.

My stilettos click under me as I make my way down the marbled hallway, quickly locking myself inside the bathroom that smells like roses.

I place my purse on the counter and text Aiden.

I'm here.

Tell me what you're wearing.

A cream wool knit dress.

Perfect. I want you to remove your panties and touch yourself.

My core clenches at his request.

Okay.

And I want you to take a picture of yourself doing it and send it to me.

What the...

Has he lost his damn mind?

I can't do that.

Do you trust me, Buzzy?

I sigh in frustration. He knows the answer as well as I do.

Of course.

Then do as I ask.

Fine, I reply, feigning annoyance but grinning mischievously to myself.

I place my phone next to my clutch, then using the wall for support, I take off my thong. I pick the phone up and send him a picture of it dangling from my index finger.

A second later...*Keep going.*

Patience.

I don't like being kept waiting.

I roll my eyes. Incorrigible man.

Swiping on my camera app, I focus it on me. Holding the phone in my left hand, I insert my index finger into my pussy and capture it.

I message him the photo. *Happy now?*

No, not at all. Now I want you to finger-fuck yourself and text me the audio of when you come.

I almost drop the phone on the floor.

He's got to be joking. I'm in Penelope Covington's guest bathroom, one of the last society matriarchs of Manhattan, and he wants me to literally fuck myself for his pleasure?

I can't.

Why not?

Because...what if I get caught?

You can do this, Buzzy. And what's more, I know deep down this excites you. Doing something so sexy and forbidden. You're more than the perfect Park Avenue Princess. You are a woman who wants to explore her sexuality. Who wants to be brought to life. And I'm the lucky bastard who gets to see you do that.

Shivers run up and down my arms. How does he know me so well?

Yes, I can do this.

That's my Buzzy.

I turn on the sink to let the water run to hide the sounds I'm about to make. Clicking on the app for voice memos, I lay my head back on the wall, now inserting two fingers. I start to massage my folds, imagining Aiden, his lush mouth clamped over mine, the smell of him, the weight of his hard body on top of me.

I begin to moan at a low volume. I push the palm of my hand down hard onto my mound to increase the pressure. Rubbing my clit with the pad of my thumb, I start thrusting my fingers in and out, the memory of Aiden's cock doing the same to me until I came so hard, screaming his name, my heart pounding, stars bursting behind my eyelids...

I gasp Aiden's name as release comes over me, my fingers soaked with my essence.

I'm soaring from the excitement, the adrenaline rushing through me. I can't stop smiling to myself.

Panting for breath, I end the voice memo. I put down the phone to wash my hands and get back into my thong.

I text the audio to Aiden. *I need to see you. Tomorrow night. Ritz-Carlton. Battery Park City. 8 PM.*

I'll be there, Buzzy.

I check my face in the mirror and reapply a fresh coat of lip gloss. With my head held high, I walk back to the dining room, all eyes focusing on me.

"Are you all right, my dear?" Penelope asks.

I flash her a prim and proper smile. "Never better, Mrs. Covington."

❧

FILING INTO MRS. COVINGTON'S PRIVATE ELEVATOR, Marisol steers me toward her. "We need to talk," she whispers under her breath.

"Not here," I murmur, nodding at the other ladies in the car with us.

Once outside on Fifth Avenue, air kisses and delicate embraces are shared among the group. A frustrated Marisol pulls me aside. "I have bad news, *chica*. I can't invest in the magazine. I talked to my parents. It's not because they're opposed to the idea because you know they adore you, but the money is tied up for another year until I turn twenty-five."

Damn.

I give her a comforting smile. "I totally understand, sweetie. I'll figure something out."

Before she can reply, my father's voice calls out behind us. "Beatrice."

We turn to see him walking toward us, a serious look across his face. "Hello, girls."

"Mr. Parker, nice to see you," Marisol greets him.

"Always a pleasure, dear. How are your parents?" he asks out of politeness.

"They're fine," she answers, but looks back at me quizzically.

"Dad, what you doing here?"

"Beatrice, I need you to come with me. I'd like to show you something."

This is odd. "How did you know lunch was over?"

"I called Penelope and her butler informed me. Marisol, you don't mind, do you?"

She slaps a fake smile across her lips. "Not at all, Mr. Parker. Beatrice, I'll see you later."

"Yeah, later." I catch her giving me the "call me" gesture with her right hand behind my father's back.

I nod in reply to her, turning to my father. "Okay, Dad. Lead the way."

THE ELEVATOR IN THE BUILDING ON MADISON AND 73RD where the office for *Park* magazine is housed still creaks like it did when I was a child. Memories come flooding back when I came here with my grandpa, holding his hand so tightly, him introducing me to the staff, telling everyone how proud he was of me.

Two decades later, the office itself has retained that musty smell, mixed with warped wood and corroding metal from the aging file cabinets. The interior hasn't changed either. A small entryway with a window where a receptionist would greet you back in the early days of the magazine sits unused now.

When my father and I walk through, the first person who greets us is Millie, an older woman who's worked at the magazine since Grandpa founded it.

"Oh my goodness. That can't be little Beatrice!" she welcomes me warmly, her warm, rotund body enveloping me in a tight hug.

"Hi, Millie. Not so little anymore," I reply.

"I can see that." Her attention switches to my father. "Good afternoon, Mr. Parker. This is a pleasant surprise."

"Lovely to see you, Millie. How are you?"

While they exchange pleasantries, I gaze around the large open space. A bank of file cabinets sits in the center, demarcating the editorial areas from the administrative side. I notice the desktop computers are older PC models, which clearly need to be updated.

My father takes my arm. "Let's go see Edward."

I follow Dad to the back of the room to the one enclosed space that serves as the editor-in-chief's office, which position is currently filled by Edward Danbury, the son of a friend of Grandpa's who took over from him after he passed away.

Sitting at his desk with the door open and holding a red pencil in his hand, he is clearly editing the next issue. Dad knocks on the doorjamb, and Edward looks up from his work and smiles at us.

"Well, hello, Parker family. This is a pleasant surprise." He rises from his chair, coming around the desk to welcome us, giving my father a handshake and me a hug.

"I hope we're not disturbing you," Dad says.

"Oh, no, not at all. Please have a seat," he says, gesturing to the two chairs in front of his desk.

Once we all settle in, Edward leans forward. "How are you? How is Mrs. Parker?"

"We're all well, thank you, Edward," Dad replies. "I brought Beatrice with me today because I thought she might want to see how the office looks now. It's been too long since she was last here."

Right, Dad. That's exactly why.

Edward clears his throat. "Yes, well, we're managing. It's not like it was when your grandfather ran the magazine." He looks over at the portrait of Grandpa hanging on the wall to the left of us. He sighs. "Times have changed. It's hard to compete with *Town & Country* and other periodicals when our own computers need to be updated."

"Of course. That's understandable. Quite the dilemma. Don't you agree, Beatrice?"

Subtle, Dad.

I nod. "Yes, I can see that." I clench my hands in frustration. "Would you mind if I walked around for a bit since it's been so long since I was here?"

Edward waves his hand at me enthusiastically. "Of course. Please. I should have a moment with your father as it is."

I step out, taking a lap around the space. I say hello to the assistant editors perusing over copy, the photo editor studying pictures on a computer monitor. But what draws my attention most are the framed covers of *Park* lining the walls like a gallery exhibit, along with shots of Grandpa smiling with various staff members.

The last picture grabs my attention. It's of Grandpa and me in his office, with him in his chair and me on top of the desk, smiling so widely. I think I'm about five, wearing a pink dress with white knee socks and black patent Mary Janes, my blond hair in pigtails. Grandpa is sitting back, his arms crossed, grinning at me as if to say: "Look at this kid. She's going places."

Suddenly, tears form in my eyes.

Am I, Grandpa? Would you be proud of me now?

A touch of someone's hand startles me. "Shall we go, sweetheart?" Dad asks.

I wipe my eyes before I turn around to face him. "Yes. Let's go."

❧

FOR THE FIRST FEW BLOCKS, DAD AND I REMAIN QUIET. As we turn onto Park Avenue, he breaks the silence. "I hope you didn't mind that."

I shake my head. "I would've minded less if you had warned me ahead of time."

"Would you have gone if I had?" he asks pointedly.

I pause. "I don't know. That was a guilt trip, Dad."

"I didn't mean it to be, and I'm sorry if it felt that way. I just wanted to remind you of your family legacy and how much the magazine meant to your grandfather."

"I thought you wanted Seb to take it over one day."

Dad sighs. "Yes, but Seb isn't exactly chomping at the bit to be a magazine editor, even though his family owns it. And if you and Porter—"

I stop short, pivoting to my father. "Don't, Dad. Just don't. I know it's what I have to do, but I can't talk about it now."

"But, Beatrice..."

"Not now, all right? Please. I just want to go home."

Silence resumes between us. The only words we utter once we get home are greetings for Isaac in the lobby and Sinclair when we walk into the apartment.

I head straight for my room, collapsing on my bed. All I want to do is rest my eyes, but then I remember I haven't checked Prose since yesterday.

When I open the app, a message awaits my attention from GalwayPlayer entitled "Yes, Sir." My mouth drops at his words as I feel myself grow wet at his fantasies of me, of what we would do together.

I rush to my desk and reply to him, the words flowing from me so naturally as if it were a habit. And I realize it is. Sharing my fantasies with him has become my addiction.

"SOMETHING NEW"

We lie tangled together, completely spent.

"I can't move," I whisper.

"I'll take that as a compliment," you reply.

"Please do, Sir."

I lean in and kiss you long and deep, then I pull back. "Now I have something for you. I think you'll enjoy it."

I begin to disentangle myself from you.

"Where are you going?" you ask. "I thought you couldn't move."

There is displeasure in your voice.

I quickly kiss you on the lips. "Trust me, Sir. You'll enjoy this."

You narrow your eyebrows at me in a mixture of confusion and curiosity.

I return to the bedroom, smacking myself on the thigh with my riding crop.

Your eyes light up at the sight and sound of the leather hitting my flesh. "Where in the hell did you get that?"

"From my riding lessons when I was a kid. The poor thing's been gathering dust ever since."

You grin wickedly at me. "I'm pleased you saved it then, baby."

I walk over to you and present it to you. "It even has a wrist hold for your convenience."

"Yes, that's very nice. Now get back on the bed," you command me.

I scurry onto the bed and lie down, chest facing up.

You try out the crop, smacking it on your palm. "You're going to enjoy this," you declare.

"Yes, I will, Sir. As I'm sure you will as well. Do you want to bind my wrists?"

"No, but put on your mask."

"Yes, Sir."

I do as I'm told and lay my head down. I'm already wet with anticipation. I take deep breaths waiting for the first touch.

Then I feel it. The soft leather on my collarbone. You trace a trail down my chest and over my belly.

"How do I look, Sir?"

"Beautiful," you reply with a deep rasp.

I can feel you moving back to my breasts. The leather circles one nipple, growing hard and pebbled with each swirl. Then you trail to the other one as I moan from your exquisite ministrations.

You breathe deeply. I imagine your heart is pounding inside your chest as much as mine is.

You deliver two swift smacks to each nipple and I moan in ecstasy. I fist the sheets with my hands, my toes curling from the sensation.

The crop moves back down my belly. I know exactly where you're heading.

Or not.

"Turn over. Show me your ass."

I quickly flip over. Oh my God, I want this so much.

You glide the crop over my buttocks, no doubt taking in the view. I steel myself for the first smack.

And then the leather lands on my soft flesh. I yell out from the impact.

"Shall I do that again?" you ask.

"*Yes, please, Sir. As much as you like.*"

Each smack on my ass makes me wetter and wetter, and now my pussy is completely soaked. I need the release. I need to come so badly.

"*I love how your skin turns so pink,*" *you declare in admiration.* "*It's gorgeous.*"

"*Thank you, Sir.*"

"*Now get on your back, baby.*"

I flip over once more. And when I feel the leather on my pussy, I scream out, "*Oh, God, yes! Please, Sir!*"

I can hear you grunt to yourself as you open my folds with the crop. "*You're glistening, baby,*" *you remark in admiration.*

"*Thank you, Sir.*"

"*Do you wish this was my cock?*"

"*I always want your cock, Sir,*" *I confess.*

"*As much as that pleases me, I'm going to make you come with this. I think you want to come, don't you, baby?*"

"*Yes, Sir. Very much.*"

"*Then you shall.*"

Before I can prepare myself, I sense the leather on my clit. You start to rub it back and forth over my swollen nub, and I start to writhe uncontrollably.

I ride the leather, clenching my thighs together. "*Yes, please, don't stop, Sir! That feels so good!*"

You smack my thighs. "*Keep your legs open,*" *you command.* "*I want to see your pussy when you come.*"

"*Yes, Sir,*" *I moan in reply.*

You place the leather back on my pussy and continue to rub it over and over. And then I lose all control as my orgasm washes over me. I ride the wave, screaming in release.

My body sinks into the bed as I pant my breaths. Suddenly, I can taste leather on my lips, and then I taste myself. I lick the leather with my tongue, savoring my essence mixed in with the soft leather.

Then I feel your body press down on the mattress as you join me. You pull me to you and kiss me hard. "*That was amazing, baby.*"

"It was," I reply breathlessly. "Thank you for that. Hands down, that was the best idea I ever had, saving that from my childhood.."

"My good girl is also very smart," you declare, running your fingers over my swollen lips.

I smile back at you. "Always."

Staring out the window of the suite Bea had reserved for us at the Ritz-Carlton, I watch as various boats and ferries sail across the Hudson River between Manhattan and New Jersey, the Statue of Liberty and Ellis Island illuminated brilliantly in the background.

I press play again on my phone. By now, I've lost count of how many times I've listened to the audio recording Bea made for me. Her moans, the moment she comes, all of those sounds make me so hard for her, desperate to sink myself inside her. Add her latest post from Prose to that, and I can hardly walk thanks to my cock turning into fucking Mt. Everest.

I know she's bound to ask me tonight why I told her to do that, and I'll give her a standard answer. But the real truth is that I wanted her to see that I could be her real-life *Galway-Player* from Prose, that she doesn't need Prose to live out her deepest fantasies. She could have me for that. Now I just need to find the right time to tell her.

The electronic buzz of the door unlocking makes me stop listening to my phone because the woman who made that recording for me, the woman who drives me fucking mad and who makes me hard at the mere thought of her, steps through the door.

She drops her bag on the floor and whips off her sunglasses. "Fucking FDR was backed up for miles," she huffs. "I told the stupid driver to take the side streets, but no, he—"

God, she's so fucking sexy when she's pissed off.

Before she can utter another word, I rush over to her and grab her face, plunging my tongue into her lush mouth, which she readily accepts.

"Mmmmm," she moans as I keep kissing her, unable to stop. I could come from that sound alone.

I finally pull away from her to catch my breath. "You're here. That's all that matters. And thank you for making sure my key was waiting for me at the front desk. Very efficient of you."

She smiles knowingly. "You're welcome, Full Ride. And speaking of, what in the hell possessed you to do that yesterday? Bored at work?"

Oh yeah, I know my Buzzy well.

"No, smartass. I was thinking about you, that's all. And why in the hell are we all the way down here?"

She nods with a raised eyebrow. "That would be a 'Yeah, right' to your first comment. As for your question, it's because nobody in my circle would be caught dead below 42nd Street. Nobody knows me down here."

I smile back at her because I knew it. That's the reason she picked Battery Park City's zip code when she chose her handle for Prose.

"So why the shades?"

"This is Manhattan, Aiden. You never know who you'll run into."

"Like a reporter from *Page Six* about you cheating on your

fake fiancé? Or is it soon-to-be fiancé? I can't keep track of this bullshit anymore."

She looks down at the floor. "Aiden, please. Don't do this. I just want it to be us now."

"Oh, right. Because I'm your big secret. Fucking someone from the bridge and tunnel crowd."

Her head snaps up, her eyes heated. "That's not fair."

Fuck this. I can bring this up later. Right now, I have more pressing matters to attend to, the greatest one pressing against the fabric of my jeans.

"Enough talking, woman," I declare.

She gasps as I push her coat off her shoulders and quickly unbutton her black silk blouse, revealing a black lace bra underneath it.

Fuck.

I stop for a minute to just take in the irresistible vision before me.

"You like?" she purrs, her eyes now relaxed and softened.

"I fucking love," I reply. "Now do the same for me."

Her brows narrow quizzically for a moment. I give her a hard stare, then I watch as her long, tapered fingers run up my shirt from my waist to my chest, finally unbuttoning the cotton fabric, one button at a time. She bites her bottom lip when some buttons don't give as quickly as others.

Fucking adorable.

She pushes the shirt off my shoulders, pulling my undershirt over my head. Her hands move to my belt buckle, then she undoes my pants slowly as we smile at each other at the sound of metal clanking when they drop to the floor.

Bea glances down at my briefs, then shifts her eyes back at me.

"You're not done yet, Buzzy."

She shakes her head amusedly, tugging hard on my underwear, my cock springing upright when released from its cotton confines.

Without even asking for a prompt, she gets down on her knees, tapping my right foot so I can take off my shoe and sock, then following through with the other.

Rising from the floor, I give her a full-blown smirk before turning toward the bed, laying myself down on it.

She clears her throat for attention, waving her hand. "Ahem. Excuse me. Are you just going to leave me standing here?"

My eyes roam over her, my cock hardening when I think of what I have planned for her. "Take off all your clothes," I command her, low and roughly.

Her soft emerald eyes harden from the tone of my voice. She swallows again in her throat, not because she is seeking attention, but from nervous anxiety.

Her eyes never leave mine as she slips out of her black leather heels, then undoes her tweed pants, removes her black lace thong, and finally, unclasps her bra.

She is left with nothing on but black silk stockings, those hold-up ones I've come to love on her.

Damn. The things they make for women these days blow my mind. Sexy as all fucking get out.

As she moves to remove one of them, I rasp, "Leave them on." I stretch my legs out in front of me, pulling them up, then letting my knees drop down, my cock now on full display. "Come to me."

She obeys me, slowly walking to the bed, then with a slide of her lovely backside, she pushes herself up, settling herself on her knees, sitting back on her heels.

I take in the image before me, her chest rising and falling, her eyes fixed on me, waiting for my next command.

"Are you wet for me, Buzzy?"

"Yes," she whispers.

"Do you want me to fuck you?"

"More than anything," she replies, her voice practically begging me.

"If you wish me to fuck you, then you will give me pleasure first. What do you think I want to you to do for me at this moment?"

She bows her head shyly. "Suck your cock."

That won't do. I want the Buzzy I know from her fantasies. "Look at me when you say that," I order her.

She raises her head, her eyes now two orbs of green fire locked on me. "Suck your cock," she replies, this time with more force and confidence.

"Good girl."

Fuck! You slipped again. Don't call her that, you moron.

I smirk to mirror my mistake, watching as she shuffles herself closer to my crotch. Gently, she reaches out for my shaft, now standing ramrod straight, ready for her soft hands and lush lips.

Looking at it as if she's seeing a penis for the first time in her life, she glides her fingers over it, feeling my cock's texture, admiring its color, the vein running up the side of it, its extended length.

Giving me a sly grin, Bea dives in, her mouth covering my dick as she begins to work my shaft, sucking me hard.

Fucking hell.

I fall back onto the pillows. Her tongue feels so smooth against my skin. She pulls back up, then licks the crown like it's a damn lollipop, and I know it won't take long for her to make me come. I don't know how much practice she's had doing this on other men, other than the time she wrote about in her fantasy, and right now, I don't give two fucks if she has. In my mind, she's saved these skills just for me, for this moment.

I reach down and run my hand through her silky hair. "That's so good, baby. Keep going."

She sucks me in again, and then she starts moaning.

Oh my God. I'm going to die right fucking now. Call time of death and tag my damn toe. Cause of death: pure fucking ecstasy.

Then she starts really working me, and I can feel the back of her throat. Her right hand pumps away at my base.

"Baby, I'm gonna come," I warn her. "If you don't want—"

And then I explode into her mouth, grunting raw and primal into the air. I sense my cock falling out of her mouth, and when I look back up at her, I see my cum splattered across her tits.

With both of us panting hard, all we have the strength to do is stare at each other. She doesn't shy away from me, her eyes focused on mine. All hints of nervousness have dissipated. She is glorious, full of fire.

Bea's hands reach out to rub my stomach, her fingers running through the dark hairs on my belly. She lays her head down quietly, kissing my skin as if in worship.

I place my hand on her hair. "Come here, baby."

She lifts her head and inches herself closer to me as I circle my legs around her protectively.

I reach up to thread my fingers through her silky locks. I roam my eyes once more over her—her emerald eyes now softened, my cum glistening on her tits, her collarbone.

"You are so beautiful," I barely manage, completely overwhelmed by the sight in front of me.

She doesn't say a word, then I see moisture gathering in the corners of her eyes. "Was that okay for you?"

She's joking, right?

I reach up to her face, pulling her closer to me so she can see straight into my unwavering eyes. "It was fucking amazing, Beatrice."

Her shoulders drop in relief, allowing herself a wide smile.

Shit, I really need to talk to her, to find out how she sees this thing going between us. There's so much we're not dealing with, but when I see that grin on her face that's aimed at me, I just can't bear to do it.

I push myself up with my elbows.

"What are you doing?" she asks, an amused lilt in her voice.

"We're going to go wash myself off you. Then I'm going to reciprocate and eat that sweet pussy of yours, and you're going to come nice and loud for me."

She offers me her hand. "I can't wait," she replies to my back as I'm tugging her hard behind me toward the marble shower of our suite.

❧ 16 ❧

BEA

“Hello, sweetheart. You got in late last night. Were you with Marisol?”

Sitting at the dining room table the next morning, my mother's question stops my hand from reaching my mouth that's holding my latte. I have a major post-coital hangover, not wanting to lose the dreamlike state I'm in, my body still loose and liquid from everything Aiden and I did last night.

All I can think about is Aiden. The look on his face when he saw himself spread all over my flesh. He was mesmerized, and I couldn't look away either. I'd never done anything like that with any other man. Somehow in that hotel suite, Aiden allowed me to express my deepest sexual fantasies, the ones that would shock my parents and Manhattan society if they ever knew what thoughts lay hidden beneath my proper exterior.

I look over at my mom in the doorway, dressed in a cream Chanel suit. I clear my throat. “Yes. We lost track of time.”

“I see. Are you doing anything this morning?”

Yes. Sexting Aiden some more pictures of me in various forms of undress.

I take a sip of coffee. "Umm, no. Why?"

"I'd like to take you somewhere."

I hang my head in disbelief.

You've got to be fucking kidding me.

"Okay, what have you and Dad cooked up? First, he springs a surprise visit on me to the *Park* offices, and now you want to take me to another mysterious destination. What is this? Divide and conquer?"

"Don't be so dramatic, dear. I thought we'd do some shopping."

Uh-huh.

"Right. And where would we go on this shopping excursion?"

"Madison Avenue, of course."

Of course. Ugh, nothing like shopping with your mom to kill your sex buzz.

"Fine. Just give me twenty minutes."

"Wonderful, dear."

I sigh. "Wonderful."

❧

Twenty-five minutes later, Mom guides us up Park Avenue, taking a left on East 77th.

Oh, fuck. No way.

I instantly know where she's taking me. "No, Mom."

"Beatrice, indulge your mother, will you? For goodness sakes, what on earth could you be afraid of?"

I look up at the sign for Vera Wang's bridal boutique.

Everything.

"Let's go in, shall we?"

Stall her. "I'll be right there. I just need a minute."

"All right, dear. Don't be long."

"I'm right behind you."

I watch my mother walk into the salon, then I rummage for my phone in my purse, punching out a quick text.

❦

"Just a little bit more, dear," Cecile, the matronly bridal salon assistant insists.

Oxygen escapes my lungs with each breath. "A little bit more until what? I pass out and you call 911?" I snap back at her.

"Beatrice sweetheart, take a breath," my mother encourages.

I grit my teeth. "I would if I could."

"There," the assistant finally declares in relief.

I look down to see my breasts pushed together, making me look like a serving wench in a rowdy 1700s English pub.

"You look lovely, dear," my future mother-in-law, Meredith Thorne, coos from where she's sitting on a chintz-upholstered settee with my mother. She arrived at the salon shortly after we did.

Co-conspirators, thy names are Margot Parker and Meredith Thorne.

"Mom, my tits are practically spilling over," I observe.

"Language, dear. They're called breasts. And since when did you start using such colorful expressions?"

I grin to myself. That distinction would go to the night Aiden Dwyer came all over said tits.

"That gown is a definite possibility," Meredith comments.

My mouth drops at her decision. I point to my chest. "Are you joking? I'm not a maid about to have some drunken sailor roger me behind the Pig and Whistle."

155

"Beatrice!" my mother shrieks in horror. "Apologize to Meredith this instant!"

I glance at Mrs. Thorne, whose eyes are now boring into mine like two gray laser beams. "I'm sorry, Meredith."

A loud voice booms in the small dressing area. *"Dios mio!"*

Four pairs of eyes turn to Marisol, standing in the doorway with her mouth agape. "Why do you look like you're about to ask me if I'd like a pint of ale and a turkey leg?"

I look up toward the ceiling and shut my eyes in silent prayer. *Thank you for sending Marisol Evangeline de la Cruz Boudreaux to me.*

I point to my best friend. "See? She agrees!"

My mother huffs. "Fine. We'll try something else."

A salon assistant walks in carrying a tray of mimosas and sparkling water. Marisol grabs a glass of the former. "Thank you. And keep them coming."

Meredith reaches into her Goyard tote, pulling out a Smythson writing pad. "Margot, I've had some wonderful ideas for the reception venue."

"Oh yes, so have I!" Mom chimes in. "I was thinking about the Metropolitan Club."

"Or even the University Club. We've been members there for years."

Suddenly, my mother grabs her forearm. "The Temple of Dendur at the Met!" she exclaims.

Meredith's eyes glaze over, overcome with emotion. "Yes! Oh my goodness! Why didn't I think of that?"

Marisol and I stare at them, one upping the ante on the other with suitable wedding venues. Marisol shakes her head, murmuring under her breath, *"Loca. Loca. Loca,"* taking a long sip of her mimosa.

I shake my head and start to wave my arms. "Hello? We're not even engaged yet!"

But my comment escapes them, with their attention now

shifted to the back issues of *Quest, Avenue,* and *Town &* *Country* that Meredith has magically pulled from her bottomless tote.

I look down once more at my breasts, the hideous gown, the pedestal I'm standing on for display.

My head rears back up in realization.

Oh my God. This is going to be my fucking life from this point on. On display for all to see with no choice in the matter. I'm a puppet at the mercy of other people's manipulations of my strings.

I turn around to Cecile, giving her a slight smile. "Could you help me down? I'd like to change."

Marisol gives me a pointed look. "And we have to talk."

"You have two more gowns to try on," Cecile informs me.

I sigh, then slap another smile on my face. "Of course. Could you get my purse for me?"

"I'll get it," Marisol offers.

Cecile holds out her hand to me to help me down from the platform. I head back for the dressing room, the crinoline under my gown swishing with every step.

I pull the train behind me inside the space. "Just let me know when you're ready for the next one," Cecile says.

Marisol steps in with my purse and mimosa. "Thank you," I tell Cecile right before I shut the door.

I flop onto the settee in the changing room, while Marisol settles in next to me, taking care while pushing my gown to the side. "Okay, *chica*. What in the fuck is going on?"

"First, give me that," I ask her, pointing at her mimosa. I take a long sip from the flute, before handing it back to her.

"Thank you. Basically, my mom asked me to go with her somewhere this morning. She didn't tell me where. Then when we turned onto 77th, I knew she was bringing me here."

"Like with your dad after that lunch taking you to the magazine office. What the hell is with your parents?"

"Damned if I know. And we're not even engaged yet. And I don't plan to be because I have other suitors."

She holds her hand up to me, palm facing front. "Whoa! Stop right there! What 'suitors'? And that's 'suitors' with an *s?*"

I nod my head, flashing her a knowing smile. "Yup. You heard correctly."

"Details, now," she demands.

I clear my throat. "Suitor number 1 is someone I met on that website I told you about."

"Prose?"

"Yeah. His username is GalwayPlayer."

She whistles. "Irish. Nice. Hopefully the player part means he's not a manwhore."

I jump in my seat. "I thought the same thing! But no, thank God. He just likes to play rugby."

"Mmmm. I'm loving the sound of him already. How are his fantasies?"

A dreamy look comes over my face.

"Never mind," she replies. "I have my answer. So, who's Suitor number 2?"

I look away from her steady gaze, steeling myself before I turn back to her and respond. "Aiden."

Her mouth drops. "Wait. Aiden, Aiden? As in Seb's best friend? As in the guy whose guts you've hated since you were eleven?"

I nod. "Yup, that Aiden."

Marisol finishes off her mimosa. "When did all of this start?"

I sigh. "Honestly, I think I've always been attracted to him, but I never wanted to admit it to myself. Maybe I loved our verbal sparring too much to even think there might be something more. And my family being who they are, I never really dated outside my circle. It never even crossed my mind.

It's like he's been in front of me all this time, slowly getting under my skin without me even realizing it."

"I can see that, especially the part about your family. I mean, look where we're sitting right now," she says, gesturing with her arms to the open space around us. "Okay, but now get to the good stuff. I need a timeline."

"We first kissed in a coat closet at the Waldorf on New Year's Eve."

Marisol's eyes widen like saucers. "At the ball? I love it! You still owe me for taking Porter off your hands."

I wave my hand at her. "Yeah, yeah, I know. I'll take you to lunch or something. After that, we had sex twice, once at his house, and once at the Ritz-Carlton downtown."

My friend claps her hands together in applause. "Yes! I love it!"

"And at the lunch, we sexted."

She points her finger at me. "Oh my God! That's why you left the room! I can't believe it. The Park Avenue Princess sexting a hot construction worker in Queens from a fancy ladies' lunch on Fifth Avenue. This is too much! Okay, now the real question. How is the sex?"

I give her a sly grin.

"And once again, I have my answer."

Suddenly, her brows furrow as she takes another sip.

"What's that look for?" I ask.

She puts the glass down on a side table. "Beatriz, would you ever consider that the amazing sex you're having with Aiden is much better in comparison to sharing your sexual fantasies with some random guy on the internet?"

"I'm not following."

"I'm getting the sense that you have more potential with Aiden than some guy you've never met before. You have the real thing with Aiden. I don't think that the Irish guy is suitor material."

I pause. "I know, but there are things I can share with GalwayPlayer that I can't with Aiden. He'd think I'm some kind of perv or something."

"Ummm, honey, you had sex with Aiden twice. And from what I'm guessing, it blew your fucking mind."

I nod.

"Okay, so having said that, don't you think Aiden would be fairly open-minded to anything you would want to try? I think he'd jump at the chance to make those fantasies real for you."

I think she may be right.

A ping sounds from Marisol's purse. She reaches for her phone, checking the screen. "Shit. I need to get home. Something's up with my mom."

"Everything okay?"

She nods in reply. "Yeah. She's probably just having artist's block or something. I help talk her off the ledge sometimes."

We both rise to our feet. Marisol takes my hand. "Look, keep putting off your parents until I can put some money into *Park* and you won't have to worry about the Thorne money. Just go along with them and this whole wedding thing. If they want to pick out china patterns at Bergdorf's, think of it as practice for the real thing."

I nod and give her a tight hug. "I will. Thanks, sweetie. I'll keep you posted."

"You'd better. And I'll start thinking of places you can take me to lunch to pay me back for today."

I laugh. "Of course you will."

Once Marisol walks out, I grab my phone from my bag. I type quickly. *Can you meet me at the Bowery Hotel tonight? 9 PM?*

Bubbles appear within seconds on the screen. *Moving north into the East Village now, are we? You're taking a risk, Buzzy,* Aiden teases me.

I smile to myself. *You're worth the risk. And there's something we need to talk about when I see you.*

My lips purse when at least a full minute passes by before he starts typing again. *There's something I need to tell you as well.*

My heart drops. *Is it bad?*

Not at all. I'll see you tonight.

I exhale a sigh of relief. *Tonight, Full Ride.*

Counting the hours, Buzzy.

Marisol is right. I need to start being honest with Aiden and GalwayPlayer, but most of all, with myself.

A soft knock sounds at the door. "Miss Parker, are you ready?"

I look into the cheval mirror in front of me, hold my head high, and smile back at myself, bursting from excitement knowing what I'm going to tell Aiden tonight.

"Yes, I'm ready."

❦ 17 ❦

AIDEN

I can't keep still. My palms are sweating. My heart is going to fucking burst out of my chest. I rush over to the minibar, whip out the tiny bottle of Jameson, and swallow the whole thing down like water, the burn of the alcohol warming my throat, giving me courage for what I'm about to do.

Any minute, I'm going to hear that door open of the suite Bea reserved for us at the Bowery, and she'll walk in, looking gorgeous as ever, that beautiful smile spread across her face. And then, I'm going to throw her life into a 180.

I'm a fucking bastard.

After our night at the Ritz-Carlton, I knew it was time to tell her everything. That night changed us both for the better and worse.

In the back of my mind, I'm praying that maybe she'll understand. Maybe she'll understand why I pretended to be someone I'm not so I could get closer to her. I want her to know that she's safe with me, that she shouldn't be ashamed of what she shared with me because she was being her true self, the self that she keeps private and isn't meant for public viewing. That I love her for everything she is.

I stop moving when I hear the key in the lock. I turn around, and there she stands, the only woman I've ever loved, that wide smile across her soft lips, which I think is even bigger today.

My Buzzy.

Fuck, shit, fuck.

She slams the door behind her, drops her tote bag, and runs to me, giving out an adorable girlish squeal. Instantly, she wraps her arms around me and kisses me so hard that I actually step back on one foot from the impact of her body hitting mine.

I accept her tongue into my mouth. I'm so hungry for her, so ravenous. I take her head between my hands to hold her steady, to savor this moment for as long as I can.

When Bea finally releases her mouth from mine, she gazes dreamily into my eyes. "Hi," she whispers.

I swallow. "Hi, yourself."

"Have you been waiting long?" she asks so sweetly.

I shake my head. "Not at all."

She steps back from me, tucking my hand into her soft one. "Come with me. I want to tell you something."

I follow her as if in a trance, slowly because I want to stop time right now. Right fucking now.

She leads me to the bedroom and sits down on the bed, patting the space next to her. I give her a slight grin to mask what's really going on inside me. I do as she asks and ease myself down. She pulls on me to sit even closer so our thighs press together.

I exhale loudly, waiting for her to take the lead.

She takes my hand again and looks directly into my eyes. "Something happened to me today, Aiden."

"What?"

"I was trying on wedding gowns with my mom and Mrs. Thorne when I had this amazing moment of clarity."

My eyes widen. "Hold on a sec. You were trying on wedding gowns? Why the fuck would you do that? I asked you to give me a chance. You're still going ahead with this bullshit marriage?"

"Hey!" she interrupts. "Could you let me finish?"

I exhale, holding her hand tighter. "Fine. Go on."

"I stood on this pedestal and watched as my wedding was being planned for me. There was Meredith, pulling out reception ideas from her bag and my mom totally swooning and getting all excited, and then it hit me. This was what my life was going to be like until I die. Everything being planned right down to the place setting and fabric swatch, being married to someone I could never love, having children only for appearances and to carry on the family name."

I simply nod, waiting for the next sentence with a huge lump in my throat.

"I don't want any of that, Aiden. And now I know what I do want."

Tears appear in the corners of her eyes.

Oh God. No. Please no.

"I want a life with you because I love you, Aiden. I love you so much. These past few weeks have made me realize what's been in front of me all this time, and I'm so sorry it took me so long to realize it. But now I know. And it's going to be you and me from now on. Buzzy and Full Ride."

I shut my eyes in pleasure and pain. Finally, the woman I've loved for far longer than I can remember tells me she loves me in return, and now, I'm going to risk that love.

"Aiden? Say something, please," she begs me, barely above a whisper. "I thought you'd be happy about this. Unless you've changed your mind..."

Her nervousness snaps me into action as I grab her face

and kiss her so hard and deep because I want her to remember this moment. "I love you, Buzzy, and I always will."

Bea's shoulders drop in relief. "Thank God for that. I was so worried for a second."

I rise to my feet and walk to the window, turning my back to her because I won't be able to bear the look on her face when I say it. I've never been more scared in my life.

"Aiden? What is it?"

"*Ecstasy*," I whisper to the window.

"What?"

"*The Confession.*"

I hear her gasp audibly.

"*Quid Pro Quo.*"

I hate myself. I hate myself.

"*A Wall-*"

"*-and a Pair of Pigalles*," she finishes for me.

I finally allow myself to turn around, holding onto the smallest amount of hope that she'll understand and see this as a good thing.

When I find the strength to look in Bea's face, all color has disappeared from it. She's paler than the rest of her creamy flesh, the flesh I've licked and kissed. Her jaw is clenched, her lips forming a straight, hard line. And her eyes, those emerald eyes that resemble freshly cut grass, are now ice cold.

"You're GalwayPlayer?" she asks, the venom potent in her voice.

I bore my eyes into hers, not hiding anything. "Yes."

"How did it start?" she hisses.

"Your laptop was open in the library that day at your family's Boxing Day dinner."

She nods in comprehension, her lips pressed together in a hard line. "You must've had some good laughs over what I wrote."

I take a step toward her. "No, baby—"

Bea thrusts her shaking hand into the air, palm facing me to keep me from coming any closer, and I obey her.

I watch as she jumps to her feet. "What were you going to do? Sell my fantasies to the highest bidder?" she snarls.

"Fuck no, Buzzy!"

"DO NOT EVER CALL ME THAT AGAIN! I want you out of my life! You're going to tell Seb that you can't be friends with him anymore. I don't give a shit what reason you give him. You are nothing but a fucking liar, some worthless piece of working class trash who's used my family long enough. I guess you finally lived up to your nickname, didn't you, Full Ride?"

I shake my head, not at all surprised that she used the class card to validate her excuse for ending things.

"You know that's bullshit, Bea!" I yell back at her roughly, too upset to keep myself in check. "Do you know why I joined Prose? Because I wanted to get to know you. I wanted to show you that I could be the man you want, the man you need. You just have to give us a chance. Please. I am so sorry that I did it this way, but those fantasies, they made me love you even more. Can't you see that?"

I can only stand by helplessly as full, body-wracking sobs overtake her body. She wraps her arms around herself to keep her steady. "Get out! Get the fuck out! I hate you, Aiden! I fucking hate you!"

Her words push me over the edge. Not only is my hope gone, but it's been replaced by anger at her, at her fucking family, her fucking world, and her cowardice in not being able to hold her head up high and admit what she truly wants.

"That's fucking fine! I'm out of here!" I shout back at her before rushing into the living area to grab my jacket, throwing the door open, and slamming it shut behind me.

The hotel guests in the elevator give me odd looks, seeing

the fury in my eyes, but I could fucking care less. When I finally make it onto the street, I inhale a gulp of air and start walking south. I cross East Houston Street when a neon sign catches my eye. I walk into the small dingy space that smells of mold and age, hauling myself onto a stool.

"Whiskey," I order from the biker chick behind the bar. "And don't stop until I'm facedown on the fucking floor."

I can't open my eyes. My eyes are glued shut. I gently touch them with my fingers.

No, they're not closed from an excess of eyelash glue.

My eyelashes are glued together thanks to the layer of salt crusted on them. I wince as I slowly peel them apart. When I finally see what's around me, I'm cocooned in a duvet, sunlight streaming through the window. I carefully unfurl myself to reveal a large red cursive *B* embroidered on it.

Where am I?

And then, it all comes back to me.

Last night. The Bowery Hotel. Aiden. GalwayPlayer.

I must've cried myself to sleep without even bothering to change because my silk blouse and wool pants are now wrinkled beyond belief.

I can barely move, my limbs lying limp on my sides like wet noodles. I stretch my legs until I feel the burn in my muscles. My strength is depleted.

I reach over to the phone on the nightstand, pressing the number for room service.

A perky assistant answers on the other end. I order a double espresso and buttered toast because that's all my stomach can handle right now.

When I spot my purse on the floor next to me, I grab it, cringing in pain.

Powering on my cell, it lights up like a Christmas tree. I have missed calls from my parents and two texts from Seb asking where I am.

I quickly call home.

"Good morning. Parker residence," Sinclair answers in his usual authoritative tone.

"Sinclair, it's me. Please tell Mom and Dad that I'm fine and that I'll call them later."

"They're having breakfast now. I can just call them to the phone," he offers.

"No, no, really. I'm okay. You can tell them that I'll be home later today."

"Very well, Miss Beatrice. Are you in need of anything?"

I smile at his concern. "No, Sinclair, but thank you."

"My pleasure."

I lie back on the soft pillows, burrowing once again into the duvet.

Aiden's face won't escape my mind.

Queens. Ha! As if I could really live there. I'm a Parker. Parkers live in Manhattan on Park Avenue.

In the end, Aiden didn't know me at all, not the real Beatrice Parker. He knew 10280girl. She was a façade. There was nothing real about her.

I come from an important family, and I'm destined for great things, not to be some construction worker's wife in Astoria. Please. I'm going to be engaged to the son from one of the most prominent society families in Manhattan.

I grab my phone once more. I google the schedule for

Acela trains to Boston and book myself a ticket, then I text Marisol.

THREE SHARP KNOCKS AT THE DOOR ALMOST MAKE ME SPILL my espresso all over the white hotel robe I'm wearing.

I pad to the door, revealing Marisol on the other side, panting and holding her phone screen out to me with the text I sent her: *911! Bowery Hotel.*

"Christ, Bea, it's one thing to send a 911 to meet you at Vera Wang. But for your booty call, couldn't you have met him someplace closer to us like the Carlyle or the Mark? Since when do you go below 42nd Street? And you ask for a fresh set of clothes! And you know it's rush hour so Uber charges..."

She stops talking when she takes a longer look at me, seeing my bloodshot eyes and pale face.

"Oh, fuck," she whispers before pulling me into a tight hug. She takes me by the elbow, leading me to the love seat in the living area where she settles me down, dumps a tote bag on the floor, and grabs the bottled water that came with my coffee.

I tuck myself into the robe, ready for her questions.

"What happened, *chica*?"

I blurt it out. "Aiden is GalwayPlayer."

She shakes her head in confusion. "Wait a sec. The guy you've been writing to on that website is Aiden?"

I nod silently.

"What...How?"

I take a deep breath. "Apparently, he saw the site open on my laptop the day he came over for dinner after Christmas. Then he joined Prose to get to know the real me, so I could see that he was the right man for me."

"Oh my God," she mutters under her breath. "What happened after he told you?"

I laugh derisively. "What do you think? I told him I hated him and I never wanted to see him again. He actually had the nerve to tell me he loved me."

"He did, huh?"

"Yeah."

"Hmmm," she murmurs contemplatively.

"What?"

"Forgive me for playing devil's advocate here, but don't you think his heart was in the right place? You've been at each other's throats for all these years, so you didn't exactly make it easy for him. He wanted you to let him in, and you did. Okay, granted, it wasn't the best way, but now he *does* know you, the real you. Don't you think that it's worth a shot with him?"

I shake my head vehemently. "He lied to me, Marisol. He *lied*. I let myself be vulnerable with him, and now he's humiliated me. I can't see past that."

She replies with an exasperated sigh. "Fine. Then what now?"

"I'm taking the noon Acela train to Boston to talk to Porter."

Marisol leans back in shock. "Don't tell me you're going to go through with the wedding?"

I take a final sip of my espresso, rising to my feet. "Yes, I am. I can't believe how stupid I was, joining that fucking website. What did it get me?"

She jumps up from the love seat, her eyes fiery. "It brought you the love of your life, Beatriz! I can't believe how stubborn you're being. So what if he wasn't raised on Park Avenue? So what if he didn't go to the proper schools? I get that your pride is hurt, but he loves you, *chica*. Do you know how fucking rare that is?"

I do.

I clench my fists, willing myself to remain strong "Look, it just wasn't meant to be. And I'm going to take over the magazine. Hopefully, it'll give me some purpose in life besides being the perfect wife and mother. I have to go shower."

"Ugh! Fine!" my best friend growls at me. "Even though you're being completely *loca,* I still love you. And while you're in the shower, I'm going to invade your minibar and it's all going on your bill for dragging me downtown at this ungodly hour."

"That's fair," I concur.

I turn around to head for the bathroom when Marisol's voice calls me back. "Are you sure about this?"

"Yes," I instantly reply.

Like I have a fucking choice.

❧

"Name?" the young security guard asks.

I pull out my passport. "Beatrice Parker. I'm Porter Thorne's fiancée."

He glances at my photo, then me, picking up the phone on the desk. "Just a sec... Professor Thorne, a Beatrice Parker is here to see you...Okay."

The guard hangs up the phone. "Go on back. Third door on the left."

"Thank you."

The white cold concrete hallway matches the exterior of the building—drab and impersonal.

I knock on the door. Porter opens it dressed like what I would expect—white lab coat, pocket protector lined with pens, glasses that need cleaning on the bridge of his nose, which I watch him push up after he opens the door.

"Beatrice. This is a surprise. Is everything all right?"

"Could we talk?"

"Ummm...yeah...sure...of course," he stammers. "Let's go into my office."

I follow him, mesmerized by everything around me—the other men and women dressed the same as him, microscopes and notebooks strewn about on black marble-topped tables, and the sound of liquid bubbling in beakers over Bunsen burners.

We end up in a small, cramped, windowless office. Bookshelves are crammed, file folders piled high on his desk.

He picks up a dog-eared collection of *Scientific American* off the chair opposite his desk, offering the now-empty seat to me. "Please."

I settle myself in while he sits in his desk chair. "What's going on?"

I clear my throat. "I'm here to apologize. I wasn't the nicest person when our parents brought us together, and I feel badly about that."

He gives me a quick smile. "It's okay. You were getting your revenge on all those times I stepped on your feet in dance class."

I laugh to myself. "You're kind to say that. Look, I'm going to cut to the chase. I think we should go through with the wedding."

His eyes widen in surprise. "You do?"

I nod. "Yes. We both love our families and we want to do what's right, don't we?"

"I agree," he replies cautiously, "but what about my work here?"

"I wouldn't stand in your way. I know your research is important to you, so you can spend as much time as you need here, and I'll be back in Manhattan."

Porter leans back in his chair, looking at me curiously. "What about that guy who was at the ball?"

I bite down on the inside of my lower lip. "You don't need to worry about him. He's no longer in my life."

He watches me for a full minute. "Beatrice, are you sure about this? You were so adamantly opposed to the marriage when our parents got us together."

"I am sure. One hundred percent."

He twitches his head. "Huh. Well, all right then." He tugs on his desk drawer, searching for something. He hands me a business card. "This is all of my information. You don't need to consult me about anything regarding the wedding. Just tell me when and where to show up. I'm sure our mothers will handle the rest."

I glance up at him, the image of our mothers back at Vera Wang crossing my mind—conferring, plotting, micromanaging.

I smile as warmly as I can at him. "You have no idea."

He rises to his feet. "Very well, then. Let me walk you out."

I follow him once more as he leads me to the door. Right before I step through the doorway, he calls my name. When I turn back around, Porter leans in and kisses me on the cheek. "It was good to see you."

"Thank you. You too."

Walking past the guard, I step outside and grab my phone to call for an Uber, which arrives in five minutes.

"South Station. Acela," I tell the driver.

"Yes, ma'am." He glances at me in the mirror. "Are you all right?"

"Why do you ask?"

He gestures to his face and runs his index finger down his cheek.

I pull out my compact. Dried streams of tears trail down my face, tears I hadn't realized I'd cried after I left Porter's office.

I reach for a tissue, wiping away the remnants. "I'm fine. Never better."

❧ 19 ❧

AIDEN

"You look like total shit, man."

I look like shit because I am a shit. The biggest shit on the motherfucking planet.

"Thanks for the news flash, Joe," I mumble at my foreman while reading over inspection reports.

"You're welcome," he replies gruffly, pouring himself a coffee from the warm pot in the office trailer. "What happened, son?"

He wants to know what happened. A few days ago, I lost the only woman I ever loved. The morning after Bea told me to stay away from her, I woke up with vague memories of the night before at the bar. All I remember is a woman in a black tank top and ripped jeans asking me where I lived and bundling me into a cab, my father's arm around my shoulders, and my wasted body collapsing on my bed.

That's what fucking happened.

"Nothing."

Suddenly, a gust of wind shakes the trailer, enough to make the coffee in the carafe swish around.

"That's not good," Joe observes.

177

"Yeah, no kidding," I chime in.

Another gust hits us, the trailer creaking in places from the shock.

Shit. "Yup, that's it. Call it, Joe."

He reaches around to his back jeans pocket, pulling out his walkie. "That's it for today, guys. Stop work now. We're calling it a day."

I get up from my chair, grab my hardhat, and pat Joe on the shoulder as I head for the door. "Come on."

When we step outside, both of us look up simultaneously to see black clouds hovering in the distance.

"Go check the perimeter, Joe," I order him as I put on my hat. "Everything needs to be locked down. I'm gonna check the elevator and make sure everyone comes out."

He nods. "Got it."

He rushes to the dozers and cranes. I'm about to follow him when I hear Seb's voice call my name behind me.

Before I can even greet him, the sound of bone crushing bone fills the air. Excruciating pain shoots from my nose to all the nerve endings in my skull, my eyes bursting from the shock.

I stagger to the right, cradling my nose with my hands where Seb just punched me. "Look, let me explain—"

"You fucking bastard!" he screams at me. "How could you do this to Bea? You destroyed her!"

I can taste the blood from my nose trickling down into my mouth, keeping my face low to let it run to the ground. "I did it for the right reasons."

"Fuck that shit! I just got off the phone with Marisol. She told me everything about you tricking Beatrice on that dating website, pretending to be someone else. How could you do that to her?"

"Don't you get it, Seb? I'm in love with her! This was the only way I thought I could get through to her."

"Well, you didn't think it through, did you?" he rages. "Because now she's going to marry that dickless wimp Porter Thorne, in spite of all of my and Marisol's protests. She's determined to be a martyr."

My head tilts up at Seb's revelation, with my eyes bulging in shock.

"Are you fucking kidding me?"

"I wish like hell I were."

No, don't do it, Buzzy. Please.

"She can't do that."

"Too fucking late. It's all arranged. My parents are planning the engagement party at my house as we speak." He shakes his head at me. "You were my brother, man. I trusted you. Stay away from me and never contact Beatrice again or I'll fucking kill you."

He stares me down one last time before walking away.

Fuck me. Fuck me. Fuck me.

I watch him stop at the gate and pull out his phone.

"Hey, Aiden," Joe calls.

When I turn, his face drops in shock. "Oh shit! What the fuck happened?"

"It's nothing. Let me go clean myself up."

Joe shakes his head, walkie in hand. Something's wrong. I stop walking. "Wait, what's going on?"

"Your fucking cousin. He won't come down. Says he's almost done."

I run my left hand through my hair, pulling on the roots. "For fuck's sake! Fine, I'll go get him. Go home, man."

"You need to take care of that first, kid," he counters, pointing at my bloody face.

"Yeah, well, safety comes first."

He pulls a bunch of tissues from his pocket. "Fine. Take these then, you stubborn Irishman."

I press it to my nose. "Thanks. Go home."

"You sure?"

"Yeah, I've got this."

I run to the elevator for a head count. Workers head toward me in groups. I shout out "Great job!" and "Thanks, guys!" as I pass them.

I push the buzzer for the fifth floor, cursing my cousin under my breath.

When I finally reach him, the moron is still drilling away, getting the prefab steel columns in place.

"Tommy! Tommy!"

He can't even hear me over the buzz of the drill. I stand in front of him and wave my arm, the one that's not holding the tissues to my bloody nose.

He slides his protective goggles off his face. "I'm almost done, Aiden. Shit, what happened to you?"

His eyes plead with me like a little puppy begging to please its owner.

Damn it to hell.

I sigh in exasperation. "Nothing. Look, I get it, Tommy. I really do. But when your supervisor tells you to stop, you fucking stop. The weather's turning and we can't risk you getting hurt. Do you get that?"

He pouts and drops his head. "Sorry."

I tap the top of his hardhat. "No problem, kid. Come on. Let's go home."

"Okay. Just let me grab my coffee."

I turn around as he puts the drill down on the wooden makeshift table across from us in the center of the open space.

Just as he reaches for a tall green thermos standing near the edge of the table, a huge gust of wind hits us head-on. Before I can stop its path, the thermos comes flying toward me like a bullet from a gun, hitting me smack in the chest, causing me to fall back.

Thank God the net is there... Only I realize it's not holding me like it's supposed to, and I keep falling.

I hear Tommy calling my name, everything rushing past me as I reach out to grab something, anything...

I close my eyes.

All I see is her face.

Buzzy...I'm so sorry.

20

BEA

"I'm so happy for you, Beatrice! You and Porter make a lovely couple."

"You're going to have such gorgeous children."

Yeah, we'll all be one fucking happy family.

I nod graciously at the various wishes and compliments I've received, and it's only been an hour since the apartment filled up with an onslaught of people, ranging from Porter's parents to various party professionals, all here to plan the farce, a.k.a. my engagement party. My parents make their way through the apartment engaging with everyone over pointless details, from the caterer in the kitchen to the florist in the living room, while I stand in the hallway, observing it all.

My mother steps out from the kitchen, giving me a chilly stare, no doubt upset that I'm not speaking to anyone or even smiling. I only smile when someone approaches to congratulate me. I can't even muster enough fake enthusiasm to please my parents. Truthfully, the party will be a celebration for my parents, especially my mother. A celebration of her social success, matchmaking Porter and me.

I take a long sip of my vodka and orange juice. My father gave me a look when I asked for it because it's a departure from my usual gin and tonic. I simply told him that I felt like something different. And I needed that warmth, that burn of the vodka as it ran down my throat, if only to forget the presubscribed destiny of my life. I can't wait a year until Marisol comes into her inheritance. It's not right. I'm solving the problem on my own. This is my family and I will do this for them.

The vodka also serves as an anesthetic to numb the pain when my mind wanders to Aiden and to everything that happened between us. I need to forget him, and when I think of his lies, it's easier for me to accept that we're over, but then Marisol's words come to mind, defending him and how he only lied to get to know me, and I just take another sip.

Make it go away. Wipe the slate clean. Tabula Rasa.

The sound of my cell ringing jolts me. I reach for my phone in my bag. The screen tells me it's Sebastian. When I answer, I hear a siren in the background. "Seb? Where are you? Why the hell aren't you here? I need you."

"Bea, there's been an accident," he shouts.

My heart drops like a boulder. "What happened?"

"It's Aiden. He fell from the building."

My left hand clamps over my mouth.

No. No. No. Please God, no.

"When? Where is he? Are you with him?"

"Yeah, I'm in the ambulance. We're going to New York-Presbyterian in Flushing."

My hands start to shake. "Okay, okay, okay. I'll be there as soon as I can. Just keep me posted."

I end the call, rushing to my room to grab my purse. I head for the front door when a hand reaches out and grabs my arm.

"Sweetheart, what is it?" my father asks.

"It's Aiden. He fell at the site in Long Island City."

Mom comes toward me, her eyes narrowed on us, a plastic smile across her lips. "What's going on? Everyone is looking."

That's right, Mom. Worry more about appearances than your own daughter.

"Aiden has been in an accident, Margot," my father informs her.

"Oh dear," she whispers. "Is he all right?"

I shake my head furiously. "I don't know. Seb is with him in the ambulance. I have to go."

I rush for the doorway, my parents on my heels.

"Dear, you can't go," Mom insists. "You have an entire house full of professionals planning your engagement party."

"I'm going, Mom. Deal with it."

"Your mother's right, Beatrice. You have to stay. He's just Sebastian's friend. Why do you have to be there?"

I spin around to face them. "Because I love him!"

When I turn back around, two pairs of eyes belonging to Porter's parents stare back at me, widened from shock.

"I'm sorry" is all I manage to say to them, as sincerely as I can.

Sinclair waits for me by the door, coat, scarf, and gloves in hand. I'm out the door in less than a minute. I don't have time to get an Uber. I hail a taxi and give a hundred-dollar bill to the cabbie to make him run red lights if necessary.

❧

THE INTERN RECITES AIDEN'S INJURIES TO THE RESIDENT on call.

"Aiden Dwyer, thirty years of age. Fall from a construction site. Seven broken ribs, broken collarbone, broken right leg, broken left arm, severe internal bleeding, required five units of blood during surgery, punctured lung, chest tube inserted…"

It's a scene straight out of *Grey's* fucking *Anatomy*.

I take in the sight of Aiden with needles stuck in him, tubes running everywhere, an oxygen mask over his nose, machines beeping, and a monitor with his heart rate on constant display. I want to jump up from my chair in the corner and shout at them, "He's not a goddamn science project! He's not here for you to dissect and talk about as if he weren't here! Just make him open his goddamn eyes!"

But he won't because he's in a medically induced coma due to his injuries. Thank God he's at a regional Level 1 trauma center, because otherwise, I would've spared no expense to transfer him to the best doctor in Manhattan, which probably wouldn't have been possible due to the extent of his injuries.

Instead, I'm here in Queens, Flushing to be exact. I watch as Aiden's father listens to the doctor and the interns with Seb at his side.

I've barely spoken a word since I got here. I can't say anything. I can't because I'm the reason he's lying in that bed.

When I arrived at the hospital, Seb told me that he was at the site to have it out with Aiden over me, but I'm almost glad, because he was there when Aiden fell. He called both Mr. Dwyer and me from the ambulance. Apparently, the wind knocked him over and he fell to the ground because of a faulty safety net.

But that's bullshit.

He's here because of me. Because I refused to listen to what he had to say like the stubborn bitch I am. Because I told him I never wanted to see him again. Because I broke him.

He's broken because of me.

With my brother at his side, Mr. Dwyer stands near the

doctors, absorbing every word. The doctor in charge turns to Aiden's father, explaining the necessity of the coma, how Aiden's body has experienced such extensive trauma that he needs the time to heal.

The saving grace is that he was wearing his hardhat, so his brain is completely safe. The doctor checks Aiden's reflexes every time to make sure he can move his toes and fingers, another blessing because it means his spine wasn't injured either, and he's not at risk for paralysis.

The doctors and residents shuffle out of the room. Aiden's father sinks into a chair, dropping his head in his hands. Seb grabs his shoulder and holds on.

"He's going to be okay, Sean. You heard what the doctor said. He just needs time."

Mr. Dwyer nods his head, but Seb seems unconvinced. My brother looks over at me, and I manage to give him a reassuring look, a slight smile with a small nod.

"I think you need a coffee. Why don't you come with me to the cafeteria? Beatrice can stay with Aiden."

My ears perk up at this suggestion because I haven't had a moment alone with Aiden since he was brought in. And I need time with him because I have so much to say.

I nod my head at my brother, rising to my feet. "That's a good idea, Mr. Dwyer. I promise I'll let you know if anything happens, which it won't," I encourage him, speaking the first words I've uttered in hours.

Aiden's father finally looks up at me, his face pale, his eyes red and sunken. "Thank you, my dear. I think that might be a good idea. Can I bring you back anything?"

My heart softens at his kind offer. "Tea would be lovely. Thank you."

He nods and leans in to give me a long hug, then walks out of the room with Seb.

Once the door is shut, I pull up a chair as close as I can to

Aiden's side, the metal making a harsh scraping sound against the cold tile. I sit down and take Aiden's large, strong right hand between both of mine. I run the pads of my fingers along his palm, feeling the rough calluses under my touch, so raw, so virile.

I clear my throat clogged with tears so he can hear me better. "It's me, Aiden. It's Buzzy. I'm here."

I trace circles on the top of his hand, the soft down of his hair tickling my fingertips. "I'm so sorry, Aiden. This is all my fault. If I weren't so stupid, so stubborn, you wouldn't be here. I should've listened to you and given you a chance to explain. I should've given us a chance."

I brush the tears now freely falling down my face with my other hand, taking a deep breath to clear my sniffles. I take the palm of his hand and place it against my cheek so he can feel me talking to him. "You have to be okay, Aiden. You have to because we have so much to look forward to. I know now that I was just deluding myself. I know what I want. It's you, Aiden. I want you. I want to be with you because I love you. If my family disowns me, I don't give a shit. I just want to be happy. And I know we can be happy. We'll drive each other crazy, but it's what I want more than anything. A lifetime of arguing with you so we can have make-up sex after."

I smile and laugh to myself through the tears when a thought suddenly crosses my mind. Still holding his hand, I reach into my coat pocket and pull out my phone. I open the Prose app and search for my posts.

"You do know that all of my posts on Prose were about you, right? I just wanted to be sure you knew that. You're all I've ever wanted, and I never even realized that. I can be so clueless sometimes, can't I?"

I laugh. "I know. You're probably thinking, 'Fuck yes you can.' I love your dirty mouth, Aiden. I hope you know that too."

I stop talking and just watch him silently, holding his hand tighter.

I shake my head and take a deep breath. "So, maybe that dirty mind of yours will enjoy hearing this."

I unlock my phone and begin to read aloud to him.

"*Ecstasy* by 10280girl..."

21

AIDEN

Water.

I need water.

I open my eyes to discomfort, the sounds of machines emitting loud beeps, and the sight of white walls everywhere.

My father sits at my left side. "Pop," I whisper in a raw, strangled voice.

He looks up at me, tears forming in his eyes. "Jesus, Mary..."

Slowly, he rises from his chair, leaning over to kiss my forehead. "Thank God," he repeats.

"Water," I rasp.

He softly brushes my hair back. "Let me go tell the doctor you're awake first. I don't know if you can have any liquids yet."

"Okay."

Pop kisses me on the forehead again. "Be right back."

I blink my eyes and give him a smile.

I watch him leave, then turn my head to the window. It's

daylight. I can't see any tall buildings, so I have no idea where I am, but I assume I'm somewhere in Queens.

"They were out of half and half, Sean, so I got you—"

My head pivots to the door where Beatrice is standing with two Styrofoam cups in her hands. She gasps at the sight of me, her mouth dropping. The cups begin to shake in her hands as her throat catches.

Moisture begins to form in the corners of my eyes. "You'd better put those down before you drop them, Buzzy."

I can barely hear her whisper, "Oh my God."

The most beautiful sound in the whole fucking world.

My eyes never leave her, taking in her beauty as she walks to me, gently placing the cups on a side table, then turning to me, caressing my face with her right hand.

"Hi," she says with such a sweet smile.

"Hi yourself. Been here long?"

Her long, tapered fingers run softly over my stubble. "As long as you have, Full Ride."

"Which has been?"

"Four days. You're at New York-Pres in Flushing."

I snicker to myself. "Wow. The Park Avenue Princess spending all this time with the bridge-and-tunnel crowd. Call *Page Six*."

She shrugs her shoulders. "Eh. Queens isn't so bad."

My eyes grow wide. "Really? Since when?"

Bea looks away.

With the arm that's apparently not broken, I raise it to take her hand in mine. "Hey, what is it?"

She doesn't move.

"Look at me, Buzzy. What's wrong?"

She glances at the floor. "You're here because of me."

"What?"

She finally turns back to me and starts to cry full-on, my heart breaking at the sight of her. "If I hadn't have been so damn stubborn and given you a chance to explain, you wouldn't have fallen off the building."

"Let me get this straight. You think you caused me to fall off the building?"

She looks away from me, nodding furiously.

I sigh to myself.

Lord, give me strength with this woman.

"Okay. Let me ask you this. Did you have any hand in changing the weather patterns that day?"

Still not looking at me, she shakes her head.

"Were you the one who forgot to check the safety nets in the morning?"

"No," she replies, her throat clogged with tears.

"Then you didn't cause anything, baby. It was a freak accident. Shit happens on a construction site."

Finally, she turns to me, her emerald eyes wet and soft with worry and pain. "I know, but this time, it happened to you, and I thought I'd lost you forever and I never had the chance to tell you that I still love you and—"

What the fuck...

I tug sharply on her hand. "Repeat that."

"Ow!"

"Woman, repeat what you just said."

"That hurt, Aiden!"

"Excuse me? *That* hurt?"

She pauses, looking down at the state of me. "Sorry. But yes, it did," she whispers.

I laugh to myself and pull on her hand again. "Say it again, Buzzy."

"Ow! I still love you."

I inhale a deep breath. "Again."

Beatrice Eleanor Parker, the woman I love more than my fucking life, leans in closer to me, her eyes still wet with tears, taking my face between her hands, staring deeply into my eyes. "I love you, Aiden. I'll always love you."

Finally.

"Kiss me, Buzzy," I order.

Her lush mouth hovers over mine momentarily, giving me a gentle brush over my lips before slowly inserting her tongue into my mouth. I accept it greedily, sucking on it as if it were sweet candy. She presses herself harder into me as I reach up to grab her hair with my good hand, pulling her into me, her perfume intoxicating my nose.

"He woke up just—"

The voice of my father fills the space of my small hospital room.

"Your son seems to be well on his way to recovery," a male voice observes, who I assume is my doctor.

I hear the sound of a closing door, my lips never leaving Bea's.

BEA

I stare at the ceiling of the guest room in the Dwyer home.

I reach over for my phone on the nightstand. 2 AM.

Aiden and I have been inseparable since the accident. His father asked me to stay with them after he was released from the hospital, which I wasn't too sure about at first because I didn't want to impede Aiden's recovery, and my persistent guilt about causing his fall didn't help either. But after a few nights with them, I knew why Sean asked me for help.

Because Aiden Dwyer, the love of my life, is a stubborn son of a bitch.

He refuses to take his pain meds even when I can see him suffering and wincing because he insists he can "handle it."

And he'll walk without his crutches when neither Sean or I aren't with him.

I turn over and try to get back to sleep when I hear a thump next door. My room shares a wall with Aiden's. I pull on my robe and slide my feet into my slippers.

The floor creaks as I make my way to Aiden. When I push the door open, I'm stunned into silence by the sight in front of me.

Aiden is sitting upright in his bed, trying to push himself off. One of his crutches is lying on the floor next to him, which is usually leaning on the nightstand next to his bed, but obviously fell when he tried to use it to get up.

And he's shirtless. When I kissed him goodnight, he had been wearing a T-shirt.

I can't believe him. "What the fuck do you think you're doing?"

"What does it look like? I have to go to the bathroom, and I didn't want to wake you."

I march the few steps to him, pointing my finger in his face. "Do not move until I get back! Am I clear?"

Something in my facial expression must've gotten through to him, because he freezes and quietly answers, "Okay."

I storm down to the kitchen and grab the biggest, sharpest knife I can find on the counter. I take it by the handle and make my way back up to his room.

When I finally reach him, I hold out the knife to him, handle first. "Here."

"Bea, what's going on?" he mutters worriedly.

"If you insist on killing yourself, then let me speed up the process for you. Or if you'd rather not, then give it to me so I can do it to myself."

"Buzzy, there's no need for melodrama..."

I explode. "This isn't fucking melodrama, Aiden! Do you know how high the risk of infection is for you right now? And what if you fall again? You can hurt yourself even worse. You are still alive only by some miracle and that goddamn hardhat you were wearing. So if you want to do things your way and not listen to your doctor, your father, or me, be my guest. Have at it. Because I'm not going to stick around to see you kill yourself. I already thought I lost you once."

I don't even realize the knife is shaking in my hand until Aiden reaches out to steady my wrist, gently unclasping my hand and taking it from me, placing it carefully on his nightstand.

"Come here," he whispers.

I sit down next to him as he takes me in his arms, holding me tightly to him. "I'm so sorry, baby. I promise I won't do that again. I love you."

"I love you too."

He pulls his head back to give me a long, soft kiss that curls my toes. "Good. Now help me to the bathroom because I really need to take a piss."

❧ 22 ❧

SIX MONTHS LATER

The West Coast of Ireland
Bea

Lying on a sheepskin rug, I run a hand over Aiden's chest, the hair in some places still growing back from being shaved for surgery. I lean in and kiss all of his scars in worship. His head lies on a pillow, one of his arms folded under his head, the other playing with my hair. A warm fire crackles in front of us, keeping us heated.

After Aiden got his doctor's approval for this trip, which his father and I insisted on before we left, he rented a cottage for us in Ireland on the outskirts of Galway, which I knew was not a mistake on his part, just a cheeky way of honoring his onscreen alter ego. It's not equipped with Wi-Fi, which I don't mind in the slightest. After the past few months, all I wanted was to be alone with Aiden far away from New York City, especially the press, after I "broke up" with Porter. That's the reason Aiden and I only check our emails once a day when we stroll down to the local pub for lunch to use their free Wi-Fi.

The cottage is whitewashed on the outside and cozy on

the inside with only one bedroom and a small kitchen and bathroom, but the living room has enough room for us to spend nights like these spread out in front of the fire and make love until the sun comes up, or until we both fall asleep from exhaustion, whichever comes first.

The only family member still talking to me is Seb. My parents will just have to accept the fact that their perfect daughter is now with an Ivy League-educated, blue-collar construction worker.

I still have to talk to Aiden about the magazine and my plans for it. Seb's taken over some of the logistics of the magazine, specifically how to best launch the transition from print to digital. It's still an uphill climb, but it turns out he's pretty clever with money when he puts his mind to it. From what Marisol has texted me, she's impressed with his devotion to the magazine, having meetings with her to discuss her future investment in *Park* and how the funds would best serve the magazine. Even though I had so many misgivings about mixing business and friendship, Marisol went over my head directly to my parents, and now she and Seb are making it work.

I run my hand over Aiden's chest.

"Aiden."

"Right here, babe."

"I've been thinking about the magazine."

"What about it?"

"Helping Sebastian. Taking over as editor. Using some of my inheritance to keep it going. Hiring some younger freelance staff to cover events. What do you think?"

He turns on his side to face me. "It sounds like you've been doing a lot of thinking."

I laugh to myself. "Yeah, I guess I have. That's the first time I've actually said all that out loud. It felt good."

"I bet it did."

"I think this is something my grandfather would want me to do. I want to make him proud."

Aiden kisses me softly. "I'm sure he would be. We also need to think about something else."

"What's that?"

"Where we're going to live."

I nod. "I know. Someplace that's convenient for both of us."

"Would you..."

"What?"

He pauses. "Would you consider Queens?"

My heart softens, tearing up at the thought of all the trips back and forth to his house when we were just fooling around, my overnight stays at the hospital, and sleeping next door to him when he was finally home.

"I don't care where we live, as long as we're together."

He gasps, grabbing his chest. "Oh my God! Call an ambulance! I'm having a heart attack! The Park Avenue Princess just confirmed she's moving to Queens!"

I smack his arm. "That's not funny, smartass!" A thought suddenly strikes me. "Come on, let's go get a nightcap at the pub."

"We were just there for lunch, baby."

"I know, but after our strenuous workout and heavy conversation, I'm in the mood for a walk."

He leans over to give me a long, deep kiss. "Whatever my Buzzy wants."

I smile wickedly to myself.

Taking Bea by the hand, we walk into the pub, packed with its regulars. A live band is playing on the small stage.

The barman greets us by name as we walk by, sliding into two empty stools.

"Order me a Bailey's over ice. I'll be right back," Bea shouts into my ear over the noise of the crowd.

"Where're you going?"

"Bathroom."

I place my order, pulling my phone out to check my email. There's a message from Seb checking in to see how we are.

I can see how much the estrangement from her parents is taking a toll on Bea. She would never admit it, but I know she's hurting. She's giving up her privileged life for me, even though she says that her trust fund is irrevocable thanks to her grandfather. But I'm determined to make her life as easy as possible and take care of her and protect her from anything and anyone that would try to hurt her.

But Seb is still my best friend. He doesn't give a shit that I don't come from money, and I have too much blackmail potential on him to ever end our friendship.

I'm glad I decided to take Bea away from everything. I needed the break as much as she did. My family was always stopping by when I was recovering, at least when Bea, my watchdog, allowed them to see me. And poor Tommy...every time he'd visit, that poor kid put up a brave front at first, but inevitably, he'd leave in tears, the guilt crushing him that he'd caused my accident, despite my efforts to convince him that he wasn't to blame.

My phone pings when a new email pops up in my inbox. From Bea. The subject line reads "From 10280girl."

I smile so widely on my face that my muscles begin to hurt. I quickly open the message.

"The Best Alarm Clock Ever"

Something is fluttering on my chest.

I awaken to see your gorgeous blue eyes staring back at me as you rub your nose, then your rough morning stubble, against my plump right breast. It tickles, but I love it. Your eyes brighten when you see I'm awake.

Fuck, that feels so good.

"Good morning, Sir," I mumble, reaching with my hand to run my fingers through your soft hair.

"Good morning, baby," you reply, murmuring under your breath right before taking my nipple into your mouth, swallowing it whole.

You start to suckle on it as I lay my head back down on the pillow and moan in pleasure, savoring the feel of your hair under my fingers and your hot mouth on my tit.

And then I sense your right hand moving down my belly to my pussy and you search for my clit, which isn't too difficult a task because I'm already drenched from your ministrations on my breast.

"Oh, fuck yes," I moan.

My entire body begins to buck as you finger-fuck me, inserting another digit as you rub my clit simultaneously.

I'm going to come so hard, but then you quickly pull your fingers out, and I whimper my disappointment.

"Please, don't stop, Sir," I beg.

I smell my essence under my nose. When I open my eyes, your index finger is tracing my bottom lip.

"Open," you command.

Without hesitation, I open my mouth and accept your fingers, sucking on them long and deep, never taking my eyes from yours.

"Good girl," you whisper in a raw voice.

I manage to mumble, "Always," in reply as I continue feasting on your fingers. I so enjoy pleasing you.

Without warning, you pull your fingers from my mouth and lean over me as you straddle my body.

"I'm going to fuck you now, baby," you declare.

"Thank you, Sir," I reply, my heart pounding in my chest from the anticipation of having you inside me.

Your cock eases seamlessly into my soaked pussy. You start thrusting inside me, pushing me farther against the headboard. I grab your thighs...so strong, so muscled, so fucking powerful, and I know I could come just from the thought of them as you pound into me.

Your primal grunts, and my screams of ecstasy, echo throughout the room. We're both so close. I look up at your face, your eyes shut from the sheer male strength of you fucking me so hard and deep, the corded veins in your neck threatening to burst from your flesh as you near your release.

I have never been more turned on, more aroused than this moment, this visual of pure male sexual power. I clench my muscles down on your cock. With one last thrust from you, I scream, shuddering from the orgasm that overcomes my entire body.

I milk your cock to the last drops of cum, watching as you growl your own orgasm.

You collapse onto me. I gently encircle you with my arms, running my fingernails over your perspired back to cool you down. Our panting breaths match in speed.

Finally, once our pulses regulate, you turn your face to mine, and I take your mouth in a very long, very wet, very deep kiss.

We finally manage to pull ourselves apart. I lean my head up to whisper into your ear, "Best alarm clock ever, Sir."

You look at me and give me a wicked grin in wordless reply, right before you clamp your mouth over mine, fusing my swollen lips with yours.

I shake my head in surprise and appreciation.

It's from this morning. Everything we did. All of it.

A warm body slides onto the stool next to me. "Hey, honey. Anything happen while I was gone?"

She innocently picks up her drink and takes a long sip. When she glances over at me, I can't wipe the damn grin off my face. I grab her head and pull her to me, kissing her long and deep.

When I pull back, she smirks at me slyly, reaching for her glass and holding it up to me as a toast. "*Sláinte.*"

The memory of that night at Flanagan's flashes in my mind. I clink my Guinness with her Bailey's. "*Sláinte,* Buzzy."

I take a long sip. The band starts to wind down the song they're singing now, which spurs me into action. I jump up from my chair, rushing for the stage before they can play something new. I hear Bea shout my name behind me.

I wave to the singer and whisper in his ear. He nods and turns back to the band to tell them what they'll be singing next.

I elbow my way through the crowd back to Bea and hold out my hand to her. "Dance with me, Buzzy."

She smiles and nods, placing her small hand in mine.

I lead her to the dance floor and take her in my arms as the singer launches into the first lines from "Irish Heartbeat."

An O of surprise forms on Bea's lips. "It's...it's that song."

"It is. We've come a long way since then, Buzzy."

"Indeed, Full Ride."

We sway back and forth to the gentle pace of the music, Bea in my arms where she belongs.

"Hey, Buzzy," I whisper in her ear.

"Hmm?"

"Will you marry me?"

She pulls back to look at me. She nods, tears in her eyes. "Yes."

Then we kiss again, as the crowd sways to the music and the band plays on.

DYING TO KNOW WHAT HAPPENS NEXT WITH BEATRICE and Aiden? Turn the page for a sneak peek at the next two books in the series!

UNBROKEN – The Prose Series – Book 2

Beatrice Parker, once known as "The Park Avenue Princess," is now married to the man of her dreams. She's deliriously happy - for the most part. Overhauling her family's failing magazine, *Park*, has given her countless distractions, and she finds herself unable to devote herself fully to her husband.

Aiden Dwyer finally landed his princess after years of pining for her, and he's determined to make her feel like she hasn't married below her social status. Unfortunately, the building he's working on is nearing completion, but plagued with problems.

The gulf between Aiden and the woman he loves keeps growing and there's only one way to remind her of all they have...with a bit of prose.

Warning: This book contains fantasies spelled out in great detail, a wife who realizes that happily-ever-after takes serious work, and a husband who will do anything to show the love of his life that he's more than happy to get dirty to prove he's all about hard work.

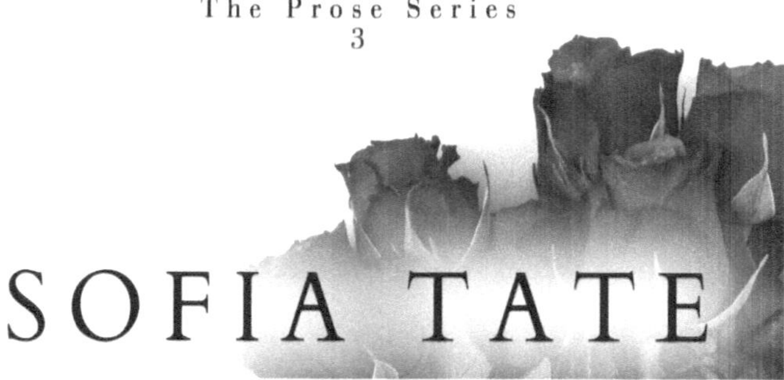

UNFORESEEN – The Prose Series – Book 3

Sebastian Parker has always had it easy – good looks, family money, women falling at his feet.

But when he realizes the love of his life is his sister's best friend, Marisol, he's at a loss for words. Literally.

Marisol Evangeline de la Cruz Boudreaux is beautiful, bold, and gives zero you-know-whats about other people's opinions of her. Seb's so enraptured when he's around her that he loses all train of thought and ability to form a coherent sentence.

To help him woo the Colombian-Cajun spitfire, he hires someone to stand in for him, a messenger to convey Seb's love for her because he can't do it himself.

Warning: This book contains an opinionated heroine who has no patience for deception, a hero who can't seem to stop stammering, and a handsome stand-in who has his own agenda. What could possibly go wrong?

TO LEARN MORE VISIT: HTTPS://SOFIATATE.COM/

The Prose Series

Unspoken

Unbroken

Unforeseen

Davison & Allegra Series

Breathless for Him

Devoted to Him

Forever with Him

Crazy for Him

Grayson & Lily Series

His Beauty

Her Beast

ACKNOWLEDGMENTS

Christa Soule Desir-I am forever grateful to you for your editing genius and suggestions to give Aiden and Bea the story they deserve. I can't wait to continue their story with you!

Jolene Perry-thank you for clearing out the cobwebs!

Anna Crosswell-you captured my vision for the cover so perfectly! It is beautiful beyond words. Thank you!

Veronica Adams-thank you so much for taking care of Team Sofia!

Lauren Smith-my bestie, thank you for your endless support, assistance, and counsel. You are my ride or die!

ABOUT THE AUTHOR

Growing up in a bilingual family in Maplewood, NJ, Sofia Tate was a shy, good girl who attended Catholic school and never misbehaved. Now, she is a proud author of contemporary erotic romance. She graduated from Marymount College in Tarrytown, NY, with a degree in International Studies and a minor in Italian. She also holds an MATESOL from New York University and an MFA in Creative Writing from Adelphi University. She has lived in London and Prague. A former resident of New York City, Sofia currently lives in New York's Hudson Valley.

Join Sofia Tate's Private Facebook Reader Group:
http://www.facebook.com/groups/SofiaTatesSirens
Sign up for Sofia's New Releases:

facebook.com/Sofia-Tate-410787962377672

twitter.com/sofiatateauthor

instagram.com/sofiatateauthor

bookbub.com/profile/sofia-tate